THE DEAD STILL HERE
SHORT STORIES

LAURA VALERI

STEPHEN F. AUSTIN STATE UNIVERSITY PRESS 2018
NACOGDOCHES, TEXAS

Stephen F. Austin State University Press
PO Box 13007, SFA Station,
Nacogdoches TX. 75962.
sfapress@sfasu.edu

Book and cover design by: Emily Townsend
Cover art by Joel Caplan

ISBN: 978-1-62288-180-2
First Edition

For Mom and Dad

CONTENTS

THIEVING MAGPIE

Her ex-husband was stealing from her.

She had followed him from Italy to America, raised his three children, cleaned his house, ironed his shirts, cooked his meals, and then, after nearly fifty years, one night he sat with her at the kitchen table while they were watching the *telegiornale*, and confessed.

"I can't take this anymore, all your fighting, all your complaints." He waved his hand as if she were only a pesky fly that kept getting into his food.

She fought a vicious legal battle to obtain the condo in Florida and for a fair amount of alimony to see her through her golden age, but finally they came to an agreement. He moved out. Then, things began to disappear.

First, the car keys from the bowl near the door went missing; then her second pair of reading glasses. Even the wedding ring, which she took off one evening, and carefully placed in the ashtray on her nightstand, vanished by the time she returned from washing her face in the bathroom.

By this time, her ex had already returned his set of keys.

"He must have a spare set," she complained on the phone to her youngest, her daughter. "You know how he is, with his fingers in everything. He probably tipped the doorman to sneak inside."

"You would have noticed if someone had broken in," reasoned her daughter, "even with the faucet running."

"So, what are you saying? That your mother is losing her mind?" Her voice went up a pitch, and she held the receiver close to her mouth in her fisted hand, as if she would as soon use that receiver to smash something as she would to talk to her daughter on the phone.

Even so, she and the ex met every so often, when neither of them could bear to be alone while the rest of the world had someone with whom to share a meal or an afternoon. They met at their favorite chain restaurants, and asked for separate tabs, mostly on Sundays and holidays, mostly to break the monotony. All the same, at every meal, she could not help but remind her ex-husband whose fault it was that they divorced.

"You left me alone for all of nine months. You went to Europe to have a grand time."

But, he said, it was because of his job, his last chance to earn real money before he got too old.

"Then you took up with that whore, that girlfriend of yours from way back."

This, he denied.

"The wedding ring is proof."

Her heart still stung thinking of that wedding band stuck in a fissure on the bottom shelf of a bookcase in her ex-husband's studio. The inner band of the ring was engraved with a date that didn't match their anniversary. He claimed the ring was his father's, but, she said, those were not the dates of her in-laws' wedding, and she found a letter, besides, from an old girlfriend of his, one he had dated when he was still a University student. In the letter, this woman, now married, now with children of her own, called her ex-husband *caro mio*, and *ciccio*.

By this point in their predictable and recurring argument, the ex-husband signaled the waiter and, after paying his half of the bill, walked out of the restaurant with a quick, impatient stride, while still she shouted her complaints at his back.

"Fifty years!" She waved her fist at him. "Fifty years and three kids."

At home, she would look through her purse and find that her eyeglass case was missing, or her stylus pen, or her pocket mirror. Every Sunday, something else left her life never to come back. Still, every Sunday, when the ex-husband called after Mass, she agreed to meet him at one of their favorite restaurants.

"Better than being alone," she explained to her oldest son on the phone. To her daughter, the youngest, she said, "Better to have someone to hate than to have no one at all."

It was after dinner, on Christmas Eve, her two sons and daughter visiting, spouses and children in tow, that the doorman called from the lobby. He found her checkbook on the ramp leading to the condo's garage. She padded down to the lobby in her felt Christmas slippers and offered the doorman a twenty-dollar tip from the pocket of her night robe.

The checkbook was twisted and torn, as if someone tried to rip it apart before throwing it from the balcony of her thirteenth floor apartment.

"It could have been a car tire," her oldest son reasoned.

"It would have tire marks on it," she argued. "And how do you explain that the checkbook went out the window? You don't think I threw it myself, do you?"

Thus, Christmas Eve ended with shouts, the children wanting to know why Grandma looked so upset. Why was Grandpa leaving so early, when baby Jesus hadn't brought the gifts yet?

She replaced all the locks of the condo. She banned the ex-husband from the building, threatening a restraining order. Their children learned to coordinate lunches and dinners from one parent's house to the other.

The daughter and younger son avoided talking about her missing things, at least to her face. Once, while she was washing dishes, she overheard her daughter confess to her brother: "You remember how she was when we brought our friends over? If a bath towel went missing, it was my friend or your girlfriend who stole it. What would my friend do with a bath towel, I asked. And Mom said, 'She's saving for a dowry.' A dowry! Thats her mind. Medieval."

But the oldest son seemed perplexed, only occasionally offering alternative theories to explain the missing objects.

Once, on their way back from a Sunday brunch, her oldest son's wife caught her reading glasses just as they were about to drop from her purse onto the sidewalk.

"Careful," the son's wife said, returning the glasses. The son looked away. The ex-husband held the son back by the elbow and whispered, too loudly, "She would have blamed me if you hadn't all seen it."

She swung around, shouting: "You know very well what you do. Don't pretend. This time it was an accident. But all the other times, I know it was you."

The next morning, she found the front tire of her car flat. Later, the mechanic pulled a long, rusty nail from between the grooves.

"It's your father," she said to the daughter on the phone. "He's so vindictive."

Her daughters responses were symphonies of sighs. Even on a long-distance phone call she could sense her daughter's eyes rolling.

In this way, years passed, and things went missing: a GPS device, a cassette tape on which she'd recorded a lesson from a University lecture, a deck of playing cards, an important letter from her lawyer, her second set of house keys, two pairs of glasses, a bathing cap, a set of ear plugs, and a new screwdriver. Objects kept leaving her house, week after week, never to return. Sensing her sons' and daughter's skepticism, and fearing their gentle pleas for her to get on medications, she no longer complained, except to the oldest son, who listened without judgment.

Twelve years later, the ex-husband died. When they entered his apartment, the daughter opened a drawer in his nightstand, and saw it brimming with old photographs and objects from her own home: a set of earrings, the key to an old locker, a moonstone pendant she had received for her first communion, a baby shoe from her firstborn, and a silver spoon from his baptism she was certain had been lost forever.

"I can't believe Mom," the daughter complained to her older brother. "To steal all those things and hide them in Dad's apartment, to make us believe her crazy story."

ROAD KILL

Jud knows a lot about Corey that would seem irrelevant in the scheme of things, as for instance, that he wears green contact lenses, that he shaves with a manual blade because electric razors give him bumps, that his mother is a consultant for the IT industry and one of the rare few programmers who still works with C++ besides, that his daddy split when Corey was four. Corey is sixteen or maybe seventeen, a Leo, a hipster, the type who likes to wear thrift store shirts that are open at the chest to show off his pecs like in a commercial for TAG, and the girls at school don't mind seeing Corey in his shirt and his leather wrap bracelets, two, three, on his left wrist only, the left ear pierced seven times, the nostril once, with one small diamond stud that teachers at Scudsboro High won't let him wear, but that he does, anyway, pointing to the Gothic cross tattooed on his upper arm, to the Latin, *vade retro me Satana*, expecting, of course, more detention.

If Corey had stopped to consider Scudsboro, if he'd driven on 67 along the miles and miles of planted fields, corn, soy, tobacco, cotton, and pastures where the cows graze and the egrets stand tall near their piles of dung, and if he'd paid attention in town and read the church marquee that said "Without Jesus, There Would Be Hell To Pay," and if he knew that the hottest things that ever happened during a Scudsboro summer is the wind, he might have maybe opted for prep school, like his mother offered, would maybe understand why the teachers talk about him in the schoolyard when he's close enough to hear them: "They don't belong to any church," "The mother goes to Unity, bless her heart," "The kid growing up without a father like that," then Corey would know why they worry about how he doesn't seem to want to blend in like the rest of the kids, how he thrives on being the oddball, even as he still manages to avoid getting noticed by, say, the Jack Wyndhams and Mark Stoltzs of the situation, guys whose noses Jud had to bust before he got some respect. But even if he did understand it, Corey wouldn't care. It's South Georgia, a place of breath-stifling summers, of twilight gnats, river tides, and swaying marsh grass, it's church bells tolling and choirs singing, it's coal rolling on 67, State troopers on 80, eighty miles to the nearest beach on five gallons of gas, and everybody here owns a gun and loves Jesus, even the Democrats, who will lock and load standing next to their Obama lawn signs that their neighbors keep burning down, or using for hangers.

Corey is the only white boy in Scudsboro with dreadlocks. He says he's no fashionista: his hair is so kinky he can't keep it straight any other way, and besides, he says he's part Dominican, on his father's side (Jud suspects black: the flat nose, the wide nostrils, the tanned smooth skin). In Atlanta, Corey says, kids called him a douche. They slammed him against the lockers, they elbowed him to make him drop his lunch, but here in Scudsboro only the teachers care. Corey threatens to just, fuck it, shave it all off one day, there, bring it right up to Miss Marie, and fuck her and the kids in Atlanta and their pseudo-liberal dribble.

Corey says, "Cultural appropriation is where left-wing politics becomes a caricature of itself. Where's the damage? In the mind of a few privileged Ivy League talking heads whose minority card should be seized 'cause they're fucking green all over?" Corey's always talking too loud, his voice rising with every statement, his hands moving large, pointing, dropping, clenching, and pinching things that don't exist, and Jud watches it, thinking it's like a dance, what Corey does, like the way the body moves is part of the music with some of the hip-hop groups Corey listens to.

Corey says, "This sort of thing contributes to the kind of Puppet Theater politics instigated by the corporate-controlled media." He lights a joint in the parking lot because Corey thinks the principal won't know a blunt from a rolly, anyway.

"Who cares about dreadlocks, for fuck's sake?" he says, biting down on the blunt with his front teeth. "Think same-sex marriage. What do the neo-cons say, that it compromised the sanctity of marriage, right? So, what they're saying is that gay people are culturally appropriating marriage. It's all fucked, this political shit." He drills his temple with his middle finger, which is also tattooed with something that looks to Jud like a gang sign.

Jud pulls his baseball cap lower and pops another beer. He doesn't quite know why he even listens to Corey. It's not as if Corey's ideas are interesting or even surprising. Each time Corey says fuck it feels to Jud like someone gave him a wedgie.

For Jud, Corey is reality TV, something so gross that you can't help watching because there's nothing else worth turning the channel for.

Corey says, "Am I right?" hands open, like a shyster from a Tarantino movie.

"You're full of crap," says Jud. Can't even bring himself to say shit, which is what he really wants to say, because Nana's got it drilled into him so much she'd slap him across the face. Nana doesn't get worked up about much, but things like language really set her off, and, well, Jud respects Nana, which is more than he can say about his own mother, who left his Dad for some truck-tire salesman in Alabama right after Dad's wood chipper accident.

Corey sucks on his blunt with his left eye squinting, his nostrils folding in. He holds in the smoke and nods as he hands it over to Jud, who is supposed to be in History right now, who has rugby practice at four and will surely be kicked off the team if he misses it again. But he has to admit it gives him a bit of a thrill, coach threatening to kick him out: and it's not because he doesn't love rugby– he loves crunching bones without having to apologize – but it's because it will make Pops angry, like it might be possible for him to drop his Jud essence like dirty socks, and become something different than the kid who works on his F-350 truck with Pops every Sunday afternoon, the kid with the catylectic converter and the diesel fuel pump tricked up to run tracks with the boys.

He squints at Corey through the smoke between them, and Corey squints back at him like he understands, and this makes Jud want to run over Corey's Euro-cool motorcycle with his truck. It had to be a Ducati Hypermotor, an expensive Euro-import that fits in Scudsboro like Satan fits in at a church potluck. Jud feels personally offended that Corey owns one of the most gorgeous bikes ever made.

"Present from the old man. To make up for the fact that he's never around." But Jud thinks the bike is weed money.

It's Jud's turn on the blunt. It's wet, but he puts it between his lips all the same and nods back at Corey, who laughs like he knows something Jud doesn't. But then, it's Casey and Julia and Michelle crossing the parking lot, their giggles and talks rising suddenly above the mockingbird that's been screeching at them to get out from under the tree for the last twenty minutes. Jud feels a clutching in his stomach seeing Michelle. Corey waves like it's Algebra and he's got a question for the teacher that'll make him look smart.

"Hey, ladies."

The ladies wave back. They say "Hi Corey, hi Jud." Jud nods.

Rugby is in an hour and he's missing History, and he's guzzling beer and smoking pot, which would make it better for Jud to miss practice than to show up stoned and drunk. To Corey, he says, "Hey, don't fuck with Michelle, okay?"

Corey's got his back to him, arms open like he's Jesus welcoming sinners.

"Hey, you hear me? Not Michelle, okay?"

Corey makes like he doesn't hear it. By then the girls are too close for Jud to keep going, and Corey's going at them with the smile of a prophet. Jud crushes the beer can and throws it out to the garbage in a perfect hoop shot.

Jud tries to pretend not to see Michelle, but she shows him her teeth in a pretend smile, so he grins. It was Jud's fault they broke up again. Out on the bed of his truck, all things good, his hands on her flat stomach, then up, under her bra, her pepperoni pizza breath on his face: "Slow down, come on, Jud, I'm not ready for that."

He sat up and lit up a stick, Michelle's saliva still in his mouth, and said, "You look like a whore in that top. What did you wear that for if you don't want to do it?"

"What are you talking about?"

"Come on, it's written all over you. Were you hoping he'd come tonight?"

"Who?"

"I saw your text to him. I was standing right there."

Michelle slipped off the truck bed, pulling on her jacket.

"Hey!" He jumped off the truck after her.

"You're a real asshole. Get off the booze, Jud. You're turning into your Pops."

Now it all seems to him like a bad TV show, that cliché that Corey's always said he is, except he did grab Michelle's hair. He tugged on it hard, like Pops with Nana: "What did you say? What the hell is that supposed to mean?" And the kind of shit he thought he should say.

It was, really, just the bourbon. He threw up an hour later, his truck parked sideways on Nana's hydrangeas, and Jud with his face to the lawn, tasting dirt.

Michelle's dad called Pops when she showed up home with a bruise on her lip, and he threatened to drive over with his shotgun. The whole business ended up in a lot of screaming on both ends.

But Michelle struts up to him like nothing happened, pulling her cheerleading jacket tight like it's cold, though it's really only October, and it's eighty degrees, and they're all wearing flip-flops except her. She's got her cheerleader uniform. Her long, tanned legs so nicely defined, her calf muscles flexing out of ankle socks so perfect it makes Jud want to start it up again. Julia and Casey pull Corey in a bear hug. Michelle's lip looks normal now.

She says, "Hey." He nods and sucks on the blunt.

"Pops know you're doing that?"

He shrugs again. *Fuck you, Michelle. Fuck you, fuck you, fuck you.*

"Your old man still mad at me?"

"Pretty much," she says. She turns to look over at Casey and Julia, who are still wrapped around Corey, then, "Yeah, you'd better not show up anytime soon."

Jud shrugs and looks away as he pulls on the joint. He wishes he could say something about what an asshole he was, wishes he had that kind of courage: he really is turning into Pops.

At home, he walks on eggshells all the time. Didn't used to be like that. Jud remembers how when he was a kid, his Paw Paw was the smartest man in the world. Jud loved to quiz him on Civil War trivia.

"Hey Pops, what's the bloodiest battle in the civil war."

"Battle of Antietam, September 17, 1862. Give me a hard one."

"Okay, uh, what's the capital of Cincinnati."

"Hey, Jud?"

"Yeah, Pops?"

"Tits on a bird is what you are. Get me a beer."

These days Pops can't make it past noon without staggering, and by evening something sets him off, his burger, his beer, his cigarettes, the game on TV, Goddamnit, fists tearing down Jud's wrestling trophies, Jud's Nascar posters, till Nana rushes after him in her floral cotton nightgown and then Pops turns it on her.

This is the thing about Jud. He's the kind of kid that Pops would say is the right kind of American: good Christian, Georgia born and bred, cruises his F-350 weekends afternoon downtown, picks cotton for pay in the summer, wrestling champion, rugby champion. He can hold Pops down, for a while at least, but he won't beat on the old man.

What seemed like ages ago, Jud accepted Jesus as his personal Lord and Savior. He hates the way that sounds, now, like he was always that kid with the button-up sweater and a Bible in his backpack. It wasn't like he'd ever taken that whole Jesus thing seriously. He went to church because of Nana, because he figured if she could get up at six to make him scrambled eggs or peanut butter sandwiches every day that God puts on earth, then he could Goddamnwell stand it to get up on Sunday and take her to church. But one of those morning following one of Pop's nights, he was shaving, looking at the bruise Pops put on his cheek. Nana had the radio on, and Peter Frampton sang *and you don't even know wrong from right*, and no matter what, he just couldn't see it, couldn't see Jesus, Heaven, the whole thing, not with Pops like he is, one day helping Jud rig his diesel truck, or taking him out to the river for bass, and another busting down his bedroom door smelling like an overturned keg. Goddamned son of a bitch.

He looked into the mirror and said, "Fuck you, God. I'm going to hell."

A cold black feeling slid inside him, then, took a hold of him, got into his lungs and into his bloodstream. He can't explain why he slammed his forehead hard against the bathroom mirror, cracking it, leaving a streak of blood there for Nana to clean up. He twisted with spasm, his face half covered in shaving cream, his tongue swollen in his mouth, the dread coming over him: he was going to hell.

He stayed flat on the bathroom floor, like that, his hands over his heart, howling, an unrelenting fear clutching him, a barrage of knocks shaking the door, "Son? Open the door, son? What the hell's gotten into you? Open the door or I'll bust it down."

That's what it took to save him.

He told the story to Corey back when he still believed Jesus was speaking through him, when he could see it like Nana said it should be, the spirit moving through the trees, through the swaying marsh grass: for a while at least, Jud could see it. He could feel the Spirit coming over him with just a gust of the hot breeze, with only a blessing of sunshine. He could see Jesus in the moths dancing over the river, could hear it in the crab holes popping when the tide came in. Jesus, in the red clay, in the wiregrass, and in the Spanish moss draping the Southern oaks – Jesus burning in every breath.

Corey, at that time, was seeing his cousin Ashley. Jud walked right up to their sleeping porch, one Sunday. He knocked on the front door, standing there under the wind chimes, Rufus barking and barking, scratching his nails on the other side. He stood for twenty minutes in the August heat until Ashley opened, and Rufus jumped on him and licked his face, Jud dignified, in his clean clothes, pressed jeans, ironed golf shirt, his hair combed back and his chin shaved clean.

"Hey, Jud? It's like eight in the morning."

He pretended not to notice Ashley's dead breath, her puffy eyes, the way she kept squinting at him, then back into the hall where Corey lurked (Jud could only see the occasional ember glow and curl of smoke), her cotton robe reeking of dog and old underwear, her bare foot scratching her calf.

Jud told her about that time he cursed God, and then about that Sunday only three months later when the pastor put his hands on his head, compelled Satan to leave him, shouting, "Do you renounce sin? Do you take Jesus as your personal Lord and Savior?" a voice so booming that it overwhelmed the buzzing in his head, over all that singing, "Bless you, brother," all those warm hands on him making him light-headed. His stomach clenched as if he could just rise up and float to Heaven with a little push. Jud felt it, a jolting charge that had him bucking and flailing, his head going this way and that, his eyes rolling inside his skull, while his church brothers and sisters held him, singing, Hallelujah.

When the Holy Spirit came into him, Jud cried, the weight of his fear lifting, and in its place a fire in his heart, love, this love Jud had never felt, not like with girls or with Nana, not like that, a love that was contained in itself, the means and the end.

Corey said, "You did it to yourself. The whole thing. You can't scare yourself to shit that you don't believe unless you believe it, you fuck."

Then Corey said, "You're a fucking cliché, buddy. Your truck, your Jesus, your tobacco chewing: you're the Aunt Jemima syrup label, buddy, face it."

Jud followed him around for a month, his mouth full of Bible verses. He thought Jesus was making him do it, but now when he thinks about it, he doesn't know, really, what made him follow Corey like that. A feeling inside gnawing away at him. Always in the wrong places, Corey was, in the parking lot when he should be in English, playing Frisbee when he should be in Study Hall, Corey riding his bike down 80, "Come on, Jesus boy," Jud hanging onto the backseat, stiff like a corpse, the wind so hard it hurt, trying to lean in when Corey leaned in, like Corey taught him, the road swallowing them, speed getting them high, and Jud knew that he was running, but he would never get there, never where Corey was, up ahead, waving back at him. "Wasn't that dope?"

Jud told Corey about his dad, about how he got his hand caught in the wood chipper, then the drinking, the DUI, and the accident down by the old railroad, the girl with two broken lips and a smashed wrist, also drunk driving, under age and without a license. "They say everything happens for a reason," he said to Corey. "But I just can't see no reason in this." To which Corey had nothing more to say than "Listen to this shit, dude, it's dope," some French guy rapping through his smart phone. "Psy 4 de la Rime," said Corey.

It's Corey who is an advertisement in a glossy, a trailer for a movie that doesn't exist.

The Bible still sits on Jud's bedside table, but though he still goes to church every Sunday, he knows he's going to hell. There is a strange, reckless calm attached to this, like getting kicked out of rugby if he doesn't show up in the next twenty minutes.

"Let's go get something to eat," Corey says.

Michelle and Julia and Casey crowd around Corey, three of them in their cheerleading uniforms.

"I got practice," says Jud, looking back over his shoulder, like Coach might be lurking there. He passes the blunt on to Casey, who shakes her head no, then Julia, who just gives it to Corey, and it makes him feel like an ass for some reason.

"Well then, you're going to miss the party," says Corey, looking at Michelle.

It's Michelle who gets to ride on the back of Corey's bike. Julia and Casey pile up in the truck with Jud, who's got fifteen minutes to rugby practice. Casey and Julia all *ooh* and *aaah* at his front panel. "What's that?" Julia points to the switch, one of many modifications Jud worked on last summer.

"I'll show you."

Jud revs the engine, puts it in gear and rolls through the parking lot, over the median to cut off Corey and Michelle. He waits a while, slowing down, then speeding up, making sure that Corey won't try to show off, speeding up with Michelle clinging to him, her arms fast around his waist. He waits until they're on to 80, a semi on the right, and Corey behind, then he floors it and flips the switch.

"It's for tailgaters and bad drivers," he says. "To teach them manners."

Through the rearview Jud sees a cloud of black smoke blowing out the tailpipe right onto Corey and Michelle. It's perfect, the way the cloud wraps them in, swallows them.

"That was messed up," Casey says.

"Shit," Julia says, neon-blue fingernails in her mouth. "Shit," she says again, "that sucked."

"Want to see it again?" Jud says. Casey and Julia squeal, no, but Jud's already floored it, and out comes another puff. They watch as Corey tries to weave out of the cloud, Michelle hanging on to him, so that all Jud can see from the rearview is her blond ponytail flapping behind Corey's shoulder, and the hands that are clinging to Corey's jacket up front.

"You're being a jerk," says Julia.

"You mean an asshole," says Jud. "Just say it. Say what you mean.

What's the matter with the word asshole? It's part of our anatomy. Shit. Fuck. Asshole. Use real words, Julia."

Casey squeals, "What's wrong with you?"

In the rearview, Corey's revving up the Ducati, coasting next to the truck. Jud swerves a little into the other lane. Corey would rev it up, Jud can see, if Michelle weren't hanging on to his back, screaming. His helmet is dark with soot, his shirt and jacket nearly all black.

"Why are you doing this? You're being a jerk."

Jed floors it one more time, gets ready to flip on the switch, the last time for sure 'cause each time he knows he's smoking the turbo intake, the manifold, everything black. He'll have to spend another weekend with Pops to clean it out, maybe install a new drain line, too. But for now, it's all worth it to see Michelle and Corey smoked out in that black cloud.

Corey's bike rides the line between the semi and Jud's truck, a space so narrow that all it would take is for Jud to swerve even just a little and out they would go, he and Michelle, splattered all over the side of the semi, the bike shaving the road ahead. In the rearview, Corey's shouting, "Fuck you, asshole," pulling his wrists down. He's almost there, almost flush with the window, and Jud is flooring it, but the Ducati's pickup burns him. The bike veers, narrowly misses slamming into the semi and pulls in front of them. Michelle screams. Julia and Casey scream. Jud gets that cold feeling again, like when he cursed God in the bathroom. His hands sweat. His head is buzzing. Then Corey swerves in front of him, pops a wheely, Michelle, a small blackened head with a ponytail hanging on her back, and when the front tire hits the asphalt, it pops. The bike wobbles wildly, drawing larger and larger loops as it swerves this way and that, the tailpipe hitting asphalt, sending an arch of sparks ahead.

Jud braces the steering wheel of his truck. Jud pushes his foot on the brake pedal.

Just before the motorcycle rolls, the fairing scraping into the concrete, Michelle rolling and rolling, and just before he screams, "Jesus," bracing for the impact, knowing for sure he won't be saved, only one thing comes to mind.

Corey washing the pill down first with swamp juice he drove over the state line to get, lying in the back of Jud's truck, down a dirt road out by the old abandoned farm, waiting for a ghost the kids at school said came out at midnight on a full moon. "This is my church," he said. "Try it."

And Jud did swallow that pill, and there it was, that Jesus high, that feeling that even the walls loved him, that the sky was alive and Orion's belt shining with the million eyes of God above them. It was all shaking and filling, shaking and filling, thinking thoughts that Corey finished out loud and every breath gave him buoyancy.

It's all blurred, now, the way he remembers it. Corey's wet mouth, stink of cigarette and whiskey, that first, "Fuck you," pushing him back, some wrestling, a headlock, and then something in there, a decision to stick with it when Corey put his mouth down there, the fast hands, the blood rush, and then after that, only the bucking need to see it through, eyes rolling back. Oh shit. Oh fuck. Oh, shit, Corey.

PROPHECY

I

The relatives in Italy never change. They are impressed in the clay of time like figurines in an old nativity scene. Maybe a little dustier. Maybe a little rounder around the middle. And the town where they live is a miniature of itself, a Lego-land of colorful semaphores standing at the end of street poles, of flashy red signs that try, but fail, to imitate the expansive garishness of American parkways. Tiny tin cars creep slowly through impeccable asphalt lanes, Vespas buzz like metallic hornets, and the smell of fresh-baked bread permeates the mild winter air.

The relatives stand, hands on hips, and in spite of the glee that seeps from their flour-scented skin, they pretend to be heartbroken. The relatives have been abandoned. They are visited only every three years. They have been cheated of Christmases and Easters, and of gossip with neighbors and friends about grandchildren they still don't have. *What happened to our girl?* they say, speaking to the air, to the cloud, to the invisible God whose interest in their domestic affairs is indefatigable. *Gone as far as America!* The relatives have waited three years to give their good advice. What would you tell these abandoned relatives, who are lonely and so far away? They nod in their knowing way, they nod and wave their fingers, their teeth exposed, their eyes glinting with assumed wisdom, and solemnly they rebuke: *Maybe, it's good to have a good job. Maybe it's wise to own your own place. But what is a job, a house, if you don't have what counts? Eh' si! Allora!*

II

The Hotel was called Campo De Fiori, taking its name from the ancient flower market nearby. Angela and Sean entered it through a passageway of mirrors that eerily repeated a series of columns to infinity. Angela stopped to look at her myriad selves alongside Sean's infinite selves. In all of those reflections, Sean was pouting, shifting on his feet, suspicious of the man who stood behind the bell desk and of the language that he did not understand.

The face of his discontent seemed to fade as his image repeated itself into the gradually reducing reflections, but it was there nonetheless. Angela could feel its presence in all the tiny images.

She should probably not have answered the phone when he'd called her, but does one turn down a long-distance phone call? She should probably have listened to her sister, or her friend who so articulately told her, "That guy just wants to eat your heart for breakfast, lunch and dinner, OK?" But *OK*, he had come to *her*, this time. He had traveled from the U.S. all the way to Italy just to see *her*, and in the end, she had let that fact override all reason. Still, as Sean scowled into infinity, she couldn't help but think of that mirror reflection as a warning of sorts.

But then, the room had a sky-colored ceiling, lacy walls, and a frilly bedspread that covered an undersized matrimonial bed, and Sean sat at the edges of it, bouncing, only to sprint up a moment later. He wanted to take photographs, he declared. "It's nice here," he said. "I like it." He took pictures of her on the bed and near the lacy window. Then he wanted to see the rooftop terrace, which opened to a view of the Pantheon. It was sunny. "It's beautiful," he said, in a forced Italian accent, his hand cupped as if around a woman's breast. "*Roma. Italia Mangiare. Mangiare. Signorina. Pasta...*"

She clapped. "*Bravo, bravo. Molto bene.*"

The forgetfulness had, again, overcome her, like a sweet fog, blurring the fragmented edges of their tenuous past.

"*Molto bene!*" He bowed at invisible spectators.

III

Last time she had seen Sean it had been September, the miasma of Miami summers barely exhaling a breeze or two of relief. It was late. Sean might have been a vampire for all she saw of him, always at night, always on weeknights. Only occasionally they left her bedroom: if Sean was heartbroken; if he'd had a bad day at work; if he'd somehow talked to his father, whom he never forgave for divorcing his mother when he was three.

Why did she keep on seeing him? Her friends couldn't understand. He was thirty-three, but he seemed to grow more handsome with age. The folds around his mouth accentuated his manliness, making him seem experienced, sexual. He was the kind of man whose life she could never affect, so infected was he by his own dramas and adventures. And yet.

And yet, that night Sean was sitting across from her in a booth at the Starlight Diner, the only restaurant in her neighborhood still open during the hours of their secret trysts, all sorts of things had been alluded to. He called her his hot tamale. She was one of his best friends. He respected her, trusted her.

Then suddenly, "All my girls," he said, "all the ones I loved. I knew right away. They *dazzled* me." He had biographies to share, girls Angela imagined looking like thin, blonde Barbie dolls, each posing with special accessories in a collector's outfit, boxed for perpetual admiration on Sean's bedroom shelves. Harper Bazaar Barbie the journalist. Yoga Barbie from dance school in New York. Anime Barbie with pink hair and long black coattails trailing after her perpetually windswept look. That one came with a semi-automatic. She smiled at her own internal witticism, and Sean, not understanding, turned to admire a wall-art with neon tubes surrounding the painted faces of John Lennon, Jimi Hendrix, and Jim Morrison. "You know who would like this place? My mom."

"I'm seeing someone," she said. She imagined Sean's Barbies, ageless, their skins perfect and translucent, their boobs hard, perky, and plastic, the Miami way. Shadows collected in the folds of her nose, pooled on her chin under the corners of her mouth. She knew she had never been beautiful. Now she was also not getting any younger. And because Sean said nothing, she spoke fast, making up the details of her fantasy on the spot: wealthy, a collector of Chinese artifacts. Yes, he spoke Mandarin, and even a little bit of Cantonese. "He wants me to date him exclusively!" She couldn't stop peeling the label off of her beer bottle. These were the kind of impulsive attempts she made at reclaiming dignity.

Had the waitress not interrupted them with his Hickory Burger and her Mandarin Salmon Salad, she might have broken down about the lie. Really, she just wanted him to stop talking about the Barbies. But Sean squirted ketchup from a plastic bottle and said, "Well, he's nice, and good-looking, and he seems to like you a whole lot. I think the choice is easy enough."

Between sips of her beer, she mumbled, "So, you don't care?"

"Why should I care? It's your life."

"We won't be able to have sex anymore."

"So, you want to tell him to forget it just because you and I get together once in a while?" He bit into his burger. He chewed a while. "We can be friends," he added, almost conciliatory. She watched him wipe crumbs from his lips.

"Don't you care about me?"

He pointed to his chest, looking surprised.

"Right now," he said, laughing, "I'm completely indifferent to you."

IV

There was no ice to be had in Rome, not a habit Italians liked to indulge, this ice-providing business. They had only two tiny ice cubes in their respective glasses from the few she had begged from the concierge earlier. They drank their warm drinks, talking on the bed. The news at work. The cat he was given on his birthday. They rolled on the bed and hit each other with pillows. They fell off the bed with thuds then, hush, they'll kick us out of here, this is Italy, and you don't know what you're talking about, you're not really Italian, you're just faking it. Hands exploring places, fingers finding a fold, a tightening of the skin, I never fake it, baby, and things that announced themselves with the clumsiness of a kiss, that's good to know, and then just like that, all the worrying, all the crying, all the things that had to be explained tossed off with the panties and toppled glasses of warm rum and coke.

V

The best *santera* in Miami was known only by word of mouth. To see her you'd have to go to her house before six in the morning. Sometimes there were too many people and you couldn't even park in the driveway. At such times you just turned around and drove away. But if there was space, and you knocked on the door of her house, her husband shouted at you in Spanish from inside. He'd ask you to come stand by the window where he could see you, demanding what business you were about. You told him that somebody had referred you, one of his wife's clients, and if the husband believed you, and if you spoke Spanish, even a word or two, he'd let you in. He'd sit you down in his kitchen, serve you one, two, three shots of *café Cubano* loaded with sugar, and he'd talk about how he came to Miami on *the boat*, how his Cuban neighbors tried to shoot him because he had fought in the revolution on Castro's side. He'd tell you he was afraid to go out in daylight because people wanted him dead. He'd say this leaning on his knee, his voice a hiss. He'd tell you how he once owned a business, but he shut it down because his neighbors, *Cubanos, espatriados*, sped by in their cars and threw rocks at his windows (*cobardes!*) so that the clients got frightened and never came back.

Eventually, this man would take you to the living room and tell you to wait, and if you were patient and didn't drink any more *café Cubano*, then he might let you see his wife.

The *santera* was younger than you'd expect for a woman who wields live chickens for blood, for a woman who speaks to dead people and gods she calls *orishas*. She didn't wear a turban, burn incense, or look into a crystal sphere. She wore a housedress and slippers and a ponytail. She sat behind a table, a regular table, the foldable kind that you'd buy at a Walmart. In the room when you walked in you saw the *santera*, the table, the two foldable chairs, and a window. No veils, no glittery curtains, no statues or ominous wooden masks that stared at you from shady walls. Just this: the woman, the table, and the chairs.

Maybe, if you were new to this, you tried to ask how much this was going to cost you, but the *santera* placed the deck before you and asked you to cut it three times, no, not with your left hand, child, no; only with your right hand, and even if you asked her again, she'd pretend as if the money hadn't been mentioned. If you did your homework, if you knew anything about Hialeah, this Cuba within Miami where tradition and cult live side by side with Internet cafés and SUVs, maybe you'd know that a true *santera* never takes money. If you had paid attention to your friend at work who swears she doesn't believe in this shit, you'd have remembered that the *orishas* forbid their *Babalaos* to work for money. But you can give a donation for candles on the *orishas'* altars and that's a kind of payment a true *santera* would gladly accept.

Whether you remembered this or not, this *santera* laid down the cards and without asking you a single question, she told you that trip you were planning abroad, well, to be careful, child, that it might bring you a bittersweet surprise. You sat there, perplexed, scratching your chin, wondering how this woman could guess so much asking you so little, and this *santera* flipping a card, delivered another blow, telling you this man in your life that you thought had gone away was really never going away. You tried to tell this woman that there was no man in your life, but this *santera* wouldn't back off. She'd say, *The one who lost his father …the one who has a scar over his left eye…* She'd keep on piling on the details until you nodded and told her yes, you knew a man like that, maybe. At that point you felt like you had too much *café Cubano* and you wanted to get up, yeah, maybe because of the coffee, or maybe because getting what you came for turned out not to be what you thought it would be. But the *santera* talked on, and even if you insisted that it couldn't be true, even if you declared that you were through, that it was over with that man, this *santera* looked at her cards and shook her head and giggled, and finally said, *No se acabo'* (with that placid innocence of her much-too-young-priestess-of-the-*orishas* face), that the King of Hearts slept in your bed, he was drawn to your bed like a knight to the court of his king, and he would always, always come back for your bed, for the way that you (*So plain looking! So shy and modest!*) rule court in his pants. But don't you look so upset, *m'hija*, because you know the cards don't lie, and now you know what he doesn't want to tell you, and was this worth the question? This man, he's coming again, and leaving again, and coming again, and leaving again, and every time he'll break your heart, and every time there will be another woman for him to chase after, another woman to leave you for, another woman to love more than you.

Then you watched as this *santera's* hands moved from the cards to the deck, and again from the deck to the table, the space in front of you a collage of cups gaping toward stylized suns, and horned devils holding lovers in chains, and in approximately thirty minutes she would have you convinced that the life you had worked hard to control with the things you took pride in, your school degrees, your mortgage, your sensible car, had, in fact, always been just one unspoken wish ahead of you.

VI

After sex, Sean smoked, like in an old black-and-white film, his exhalations curling and drifting until the sunlight overtook them.

"I have to tell you something," he said. He pulled her head to him and held her chin with his hand. "I'm glad I called you. I'm glad I came here. I've missed you." He looked all smiles. He placed the glass gingerly on the nightstand. "How long is your winter break?"

She shrugged. She didn't want to talk about work, about papers and students and going back to Miami, where this moment with Sean might be broken and parsed with Department meetings and budget cuts.

Instead, she produced a box fancifully wrapped in a red bow and shiny paper.

"For me? I didn't know we were supposed to bring presents." He took it with both his hands and stared at the paper. "What is it?"

"Open it."

He shook it, observed its size, held it up to the light as though he could see through it. "A shirt? Is it a shirt?" He fingered the paper carefully, peeling it off from the box without ripping it.

"Oh, rip it. I don't care." She was on the bed, her knees tucked under her.

It was a silk robe. He held it up. It had a design that vaguely resembled shells.

"I love it," he said. He put it on while she mixed them rum and coke.

The phone rang. They watched it ringing together, like it belonged to that black-and-white film and someone well-dressed, a woman in a suit and a cigarette holder, might step in from out of scene to answer it. Only then did she feel embarrassed by the robe, by the careful wrapping, by the fact that she had brought a gift.

"It must be for you," she said, finally. "This is your room?"

Sean reached over her naked body to answer.

VII

Angela had a problem with relationship terminology: how to tell the difference between seeing someone and dating? Is a friend a friend if you sleep with him, and can you really call him a friend if he doesn't even know you're allergic to shellfish? How do you distinguish between a friend and a *friend*? How do you tell your *friend* that you're going out with a friend, but not *that* kind of friend, and how do you explain to your friend that you've met that kind of a *friend*?

She had frightened Sean once when she'd sent him a text calling him "pancakes." During work hours. Students coming for conference. But wait, this will only take a minute, and hold, my supervisor wants to see me, and oh, catch you after the lunch break, no wait he's gone, OK, so let me catch up, they'd gone through a list for each other: sweetie, love, honey, jellybean, baby — oh, no, that's old people's stuff! Angel face, lover, hey, this guy at a bar once called me cupcake, he screamed it at me from across the bar: Hey, cupcake! LOL, ROFL!

Then those pancakes. She must have been hungry.

He called her that same night. They had to have a talk. She hung onto the phone rubbing her eyes, her nightgown with the flower print bunched up around her waist, the bangs hanging straight up like uncooked spaghetti. Already?

"It's because of the sex," he said.

"You don't like me in bed?"

"I do. That's the problem. Sex with you is too good. We could get dependent on it. Before we know it, three years will go by, and we'll still be together. I don't want to get dependent on someone I only feel lukewarm about."

VIII

Sean curled up, his knees to his chest. He was a ball of skin, his spine showing through. He was protective with the phone, the receiver touching his lips.

"Yes, just a few hours ago...no I didn't have a chance to.... Yes...I'll tell you all about it...OK, OK..."

It was a woman. Something in his voice told her so. When he hung up, he confirmed it.

"My friend at work, Tammy. She called just to be sure I got here OK." He rolled his eyes. He sighed theatrically.

"Girlfriend?"

He shrugged. "Maybe she thinks she is."

"You must do something to make her think so."

He turned his back to her, squatted for the mini bar. "It's a work thing," he said to the bar. "It's not important."

She turned on her stomach, swallowing the questions: but why did you call me, then? I came here to work in peace, but you said you wanted to see me. Stupid questions the *santera* had already answered before she even knew to ask.

IX

High school for an ugly girl is a difficult thing, an adolescent girl with hormones in high gears, and pimples remodeling facial features. Popular girls whispering, that girl should wash more often, that girl stinks like a moose, her hair is so greasy when the wind blows it stays right into place. Gross. Yeah, but that girl is a brain. That girl will let you cheat from her if you're nice. Go knock her books down. Call her a moose. Moo, you moose. You don't need to smell her to know that she smells, just look at her face!

High school for a smart girl is a difficult thing. Tough boys wait in the parking lot with jokes, with trite teasing, *You're pretty – pretty ugly.* Boys who mock the smart, boys who despise the pimply and the flat-chested. Boys who are secretly loved by moose girls for their leather jackets and suede boots, for the cigarettes that hang defiantly between their pulpy lips even when teachers pass by, and for those girls with big boobs and halter tops the boys kiss and fondle against their poster-covered locker doors. They are loved for their undisciplined lives, for the absent fathers who let them waddle in poverty, for the overworked mothers who take no notice of their school-cutting, class-dropping, and DUIs. Boys who are admired for their lack of ambition, for their appetite for acid and sex, for their anger against those who live by and obey the rules, the shapeless, the smart moose girls who fear everything. It's an American story an Italian girl loves.

But the smart girls grow up, lose their pimples, never leave school. They get absorbed into the institutions they once thought of as prisons. They get BAs, MAs, PhDs. They publish books on the shipping industry during the Italian Renaissance, articles on the architectural influence of the Pazzi. They become tenured in the Modern Languages Department of private universities. They buy expensive shoes, wear clothes from designer boutiques, get their hair done every two weeks. The tough high school boys fade like old photographs. They become smaller and smaller, goblins dwelling in the cavelike hallways of the smart girls' minds. But once in a while one of them escapes: not a real boy, no, for that one, the incarnate one, has been betrayed by time, his leather jacket replaced by suits and ties, his halter top girlfriend a well-meaning, craft-making, part-time legal secretary and full-time mother, an able caretaker of two young children whom the boy-now-man supports on his one good sales job at a car dealership. But the goblin part of him, the one the real boy never even knew existed, permeates the membranes of the smart girl's brain, a spirit sucked out of the cave-like corridors of hellish memory into the rose-carpeted hallways of fantasy, and somehow, by accident, it takes possession of the carnal body of another man.

Before the smart girl now stands a man possessed, developed from an adolescent dream, but perfected to maturing tastes: tragically romantic as he strums his guitar on the beach, jotting down hurried lyrics of sexual politics. But he is also clever and self-made, putting himself through school by working as a music critic and as a life guard, managing to find the time to play congas for Latin talents like Gonzalo Rubalcaba and Chick Corea. When the smart woman is near this man, she is the moose girl whose books have been knocked off her arms. She wants so much not to be the moose girl; she stands before the goblin boy-man, but the boy's got his head turned the other way. If he could see her, she wouldn't want him. She's in love for as long as his face is turned away, his mouth locked onto some tragic soliloquy, his heart set on something far less available. And he never looks. He never bothers to. It's as if he can smell her under her new clothes, the old moose girl, mooning him with her cow-brown eyes…

X

They settled on a local spot, a taverna in the Fountain of Trevi area. The smell of burning wood wrapped around their clothes. They could smell roasting game on each other. It was a good smell: rosemary and oil. The restaurant was noisy with cheer, with clanging silverware and shouting waiters. It would have been a good night, but Tammy had called, like a woman, knowing how to ruin things with only her voice. Tammy had installed herself between them, hanging on their silence. What Tammy wanted was their fight, was to be felt in this restaurant through their averted glances. What Tammy wanted was to be in their conversation tonight. Angela said nothing about Tammy. She ate and said nothing, a trite, Pyrrhic victory against Tammy.

After the meal they went for a walk. It was drizzling, drops clinging to her hair. Sean held her elbow, his strides fast, his steps eating the sidewalk. He grinned at the sky, as if cursing it for Angela's hair, which was frizzy and tangled, laden with pearly drops that glittered with the streetlights. He stopped her, held her face. "Are you OK?"

The lamplight stained Sean's cheek with an oily, yellow wound. She thought about how many times her friends had wondered out loud what she saw in him. Was it only that he was beautiful? Was she really that shallow? Or was it a deep, competitive need to secure the trophy boyfriend, with abs that could crack walnuts? To make up for all her adolescent humiliations because she wasn't, had never been, pretty?

"You're obviously not OK," he said.

"Why wouldn't I be OK?" she chirped. "You're here. You came all the way from Miami, just to see me, didn't you?" She studied him carefully, for a change in his face, for guilt, for anguish at the threat of upsetting her. But no. He looked bored.

"And now," she said, "it's already ruined."

But it was a bad move, and she knew it as soon as she said it.

"Would you like me to leave? Do you want to go home? It's OK if you do. I'll be fine here by myself."

It was as simple as that, then.

She walked behind him, barely keeping up with his long strides, though she couldn't quite say how it had happened that she was following him. The beautiful things around them, it was as if Sean couldn't see: the marble Triton drinking eternally from the rock, water spouting into his secular mouth, the great column of Marcus Aurelius, the imposing, grayish facade of the church of Santa Maria in Via. They walked through centuries: the Renaissance, the Roman Empire, the Fascist era. But Sean was interested in a man pissing on the street behind a Fiat, his mouth curled downward as he glanced over his shoulder at her, as if to say, this is how you Italians do it?

They walked without touching. *Gelati. Ristorante.* Ferragamo. Valentino. Mannequins dressed in furs, in silk and gold, mannequins with blue hair and makeup watching with sightless eyes the crowds of tourists that balked at the price tags hanging from their sleeves. The streets milled with young college students, bearded Germans with huge backpacks, nuns on pilgrimage for the Vatican, but Sean and Angela were an island in the slow-moving river of people and smells, the beauty of Rome skimming over their glazed eyes.

"Look, she just wanted to make sure I got here OK," Sean suddenly barked at her, swinging around. "She's not my girlfriend. She's never been. You're wrong if you think that means anything to me, or that *she* means anything to me."

Angela thought of the *santera*, of the eerie discomfort she had felt when the woman had told her that Sean would always come back to her.

Sean yawned, nodding at the columns, at the geometrical designs of the piazza. "What is that? Something important? A monument?"

"That's a bank. Just a bank."

She half expected him to say, *Yes, Professor*, a thing between them. Sean of the grunge art picked up at garage sales. Sean of the night college classes and jam sessions heated up by cocaine and whiskey. He asked her to play the piano once. She'd studied it for five years, but within a half hour his hands were zipping up and down the keyboard, his clunky, self-assured fingers stomping improvised blues chords over her Bach arpeggios in D minor.

Sean yawned. He let his arms fall along his sides. "I'm tired, Angela. Jet lagged." He stepped a little closer to her, touched his forehead to hers. "Will you come up with me? Please? I missed you."

XI

The hotel porter recognized her, a knowing smile of neglected, yellowing teeth, eyes narrowed at the unmarried *signorina* who accompanied the gentleman up to his suite. He had looked at her ring finger, then at her ass. Still, she tipped him. For ice, she explained.

"*Ghiaccio. Vogliamo tanto ghiaccio.*" A lot of ice cubes.

And the porter, smiling, "Americans, yes? I can tell by the clothes."

As soon as they were in, Sean shed his fatigue. He wanted to buy her drinks. He wanted to take her to the opera tomorrow. He wanted to see the Roman forum. For Angela to make Tammy irrelevant was the only important thing. It wasn't about Sean at all; it was about getting back at the cow who'd spoiled their romance with just one call. She could be mad tomorrow. Tonight, she could fuck Sean, and make the fuck so memorable it would be a virus erasing Tammy from Sean's memory bank.

The concierge brought them a glass full of ice, and Angela dropped two in her glass and the rest in Sean's, laughing. "A whole bucket of ice!" Then they drank their syrupy, undiluted coke, and topped them off with vodka. When they ran out of vodka they topped them off with Sambuca. The drinks tasted like medicine. They didn't care. Angela drank Tammy up in draughts, and then she drank up her high school days, drank up all her relatives, her sister, her mom, her *nonna* and *zia…* and the moose girl, she drank her up in great quaffs.

She drowned Tammy up in her Sambuca: first she imagined little Tammy flail and flail in her glass, dumpy and wet and too chubby to come up for air, and then she drank her up. She drank Sean up, too. She was smiling with Sean in her belly. She felt pleasure even while breathing, the way the air came out of her lungs with Sean in it, floating away like a soap bubble. She was aware that she said *That's wonderful* too much, but she said it again and again, thinking it was wonderful, wonderful, wonderful. She straddled Sean and looked at him in the eyes: "He says, 'Mary, I'm comin' home to you — so sick and lonesome, I don't know what to do.'"

"That sounds familiar. Stevie Ray Vaughn?"

"No, honey, it's Langston Hughes."

"Never heard of him."

"Renaissance Harlem poet? Langston Hughes?"

"OK, Professor." He pressed her head against his chest and ran his fingers over her curves, but too late: he couldn't tell the difference between a folk song and a poem and it bothered him.

"I don't judge you," she told him. His hands seemed heavier on her skin, more protective. "I don't care about this stuff," she said. She closed her eyes, dipping into the quiet current of their lovemaking. "I love you, you know?" Her breasts perked up with that tender confession.

But Sean shifted abruptly beneath her. She opened her eyes in time to see him shake his head. He tried to lift himself on his elbows, "Angela, I... didn't mean to..." but his mouth broke at the corners, losing its shape and collapsing into deep groves.

She pushed a finger to his lips then, to prevent him from saying what she already knew.

I missed you. That's all he'd said. She had sold herself so short.

When he gently lifted her thighs off his hips, she saw herself far away, a slant of sun in that house in Hialeah, the folding table, the chair, the ordinary-looking *santera* turning over the same card, the Joker, and the Joker, and again the Joker, a self-fulfilling prophecy, like her image in the mirror next to an unhappy Sean, its curse repeating ad infinitum in her shattered, fragmented self.

LIABILITIES OF A LOVE MISGUIDED

The exultation of a touch, a spiritual transcendence via collision of lips, mouths, and tongues, fast-asleep pillow cuddles, fun sex, forgettable fun sex, disposable, forgettable fun sex, the lie of "everything will be fine," the lie of "as long as we're together," the lie of "we can fix anything," the lie of "I can handle it casual," the false idols of girls in cradles, Cinderella, Snow White, Beauty loving a Beast, grandmothers in diapers telling little girls bedtime toxic; the feeling of me, the feeling of me hanging up the phone when he calls after midnight, the deep sleep of three in the morning; the righteousness of hanging up on his drunk; the righteousness of hanging up on his weeping at three o clock in the morning; the righteousness of hanging up on his "come over, I need somebody," the dear John letters, the dear John emails that somehow go on for days, back and forth, dear John, dear Jane, dear John, punctuated with the liabilities of late night confessions, so final, so absolute dear Johns cracked enough to leave an opening, another buddy fuck, another stay for the night, it means nothing, stay for the night means everything, she means nothing to me, I just need time, panties under the couch, lipsticks missing from cabinets, a sweater, a pair of brand-new basketball shoes, an iWatch for Christmas, an expensive camera, socks never forgotten under my bed, an assortment of lace and silk underwear, waking up before I tiptoe out the door, a signature on a letter, a phone message to play over again, photographs where his face is too blurry to show to my friends, respect from friends who get tired of telling me no, not him, he eats your heart like it's cheeseburgers and fries, the other men I could have had, the kids I could have raised, my thirties, my bank account, my credit score, the trust I had in men, all of them, all of it lost now, gone.

BLESS HER HEART

When she stepped into the coffee shop, Loraine turned toward the front of the store with the feeling that someone was watching her. And there was Ms. Bartle, again, propped up straight at the window booth, her purse under her elbow and her scarf crumpled in her lap. She had the tragic look of an old stuffed doll with busted seams sitting on a dusty shelf at a consignment store.

"Lord," sighed Loraine. Ms. Bartle had begun stalking her shortly after they were introduced at Loraine's new job with ABC Siding. First there was that Greek diner, a hole in the wall so uninviting that she'd had lunch there without spotting a single person from work for weeks— until Ms. Bartle found her. Then Ms. Bartle was there every Wednesday, sitting at a corner table in the shade, licking Baklava off her fingers. Next was the bakery two MARTA stops away, where Ms. Bartle just happened to be on a Saturday morning, and again Ms. Bartle at a nail salon on the other side of town.

Of course, this coffee shop, so close to their office, was likely to be a place to run into someone she knew, but Ms. Bartle unnerved her, so immersed in her intense silences, a fixed smile on her lips as she stared.

Luckily, Jose from Logistics was here, too, paying for his espresso. Loraine recognized his scuffed bomber jacket with the American flag patched on the sleeve.

"Good morning, Jose." She waved. "Looks like we're having an office reunion." She gestured toward Ms. Bartle. "Last night, she walked three paces behind me all the way to my MARTA stop. She waited until the train showed up, then she just crossed the street and went the other way."

Jose nodded. "She's a strange lady, you know?"

"Bless her heart," Loraine said, channeling her Mother's church-speak, and feeling instantly guilty. *Bless her heart* is what Mother said to coat her pitiless judgments with a thin patina of Christian compassion. But Ms. Bartle, with her long silent stares and her habit of showing up places she wasn't expected, did not inspire compassion; only discomfort. Sure it was fun joking with the others about the sixteen cats Ms. Bartle may or may not own, or to imagine the extravagant shopping sprees the old lady indulged in at a Goodwill, collecting her mismatched suits of wool blends, cotton, and spandex. Beneath it all Loraine sensed that her co-workers were glad for Ms. Bartle's strangeness, glad that, with their professional ambitions writhing in agony on the sales floor of ABC Siding, they could at least congratulate themselves for not being so strange and pitiable like poor Ms. Bartle. For Loraine, though, Ms. Bartle exuded an undetectable smell, her loneliness and awkwardness so familiar that she felt it drip on her like mucus.

"The clock is ticking, Ms. Loraine." Jose wagged his finger imitating their Fearless Leader's tone of voice. Loraine glanced over her shoulder anxiously. Ted was that kind of boss, one who liked to lurk behind corners in the hallways to eavesdrop on conversations. Once she'd caught him emptying out her trash can after he thought she'd left, presumably to look for misprinted invoices and other evidence of her incompetence. Loraine, veiling her anger through a laughing voice, pointed out that the bookkeeper's can, Ms. Bartle's, was spilling over with crinkled papers.

"Poor Ms. Bartle." Ted sighed. "That woman's suffered such losses."

It was the poor part that set Loraine off, that same condescending pity that drove her crazy about her own mother. "Losses? That's everyone's story, Ted. Especially considering the salaries you pay."

Ted's eyes brightened behind his glasses, his fists stuffed in the pockets of his pants where he fingered what sounded like spare change. He looked toward Ms. Bartle's cubicle, mistaking Loraine's sarcasm for interest. "I'm not at liberty to share her story," he explained, "but we must be patient with dear Ms. Beatrice Bartle."

Loraine could see how he delighted in holding the key to the mystery of Ms. Bartle, exalting the banality of the woman's existence with his preacher-like stance.

Losses. What sort of losses had Ms. Bartle suffered that could possibly make her different from any other middle-aged woman working at ABC Siding? A man? A house? Alimony? Pension? What, exactly, did she lose that was so different than what Loraine had lost? She and Jared had signed divorce papers when their baby was only eighteen months old. Loraine earned a fraction of Jared's salary. Still, he paid her no alimony, and just barely enough child support to raise Lily in a modicum of comfort. The ballet lessons, the missionaries' trip to Nicaragua that would "look good on Lily's college applications" – all that had come out of her own pocket. If anyone deserved pity, it certainly wasn't Ms. Bea Bartle.

"She's staring at you," Jose pointed out. Ms. Bartle was mooning her with her dull, wet eyes. He leaned over and wiggled his eyebrows. "Maybe she's sweet on you, eh? She kind of cute, like an old cat." He winked, and nudged her as he showed her the clock on his cell phone. He then headed out.

By the entrance booth, Ms. Bartle sat in silence, wedged between table and seat, molding under a pale veil of sunshine.

"Loraine?" the barista called out. "Do you need a carrier for these?"

"There's only one of me," Loraine chirped, twirling her fingers.

With an exhausted pout, the barista assembled a recyclable four-cup container. Loraine secured her purse strap, then took the container with the four coffees and the double espresso, sliding it precariously in the middle of the four coffees. She glanced back to the window seat, but Ms. Bartle was gone.

It was 8:25. Loraine hurried out of the coffee house. A peripheral movement directed her attention behind her. It was Ms. Bartle, of course.

"Good morning, Ms. Bartle," Loraine called out.

Ms. Bartle did her best to look surprised. "Oh, Ms. Lovell." She laughed half-heartedly, a hand to her heart. "I thought…Oh, goodness, Lord knows what I thought."

"You can call me Loraine."

"Oh, sure, sure. And you can call me Bea."

Ms. Bartle stuck her chin out, her tiny teeth gleaming. She was expecting something, maybe an acknowledgment of a cozy, shared past between them that did not exist.

Loraine proffered the coffee container. "Well, how about you help me with these coffees, Bea?"

Loraine had expected her to take the espresso wedged with the four coffees, but Ms. Bartle pushed her glasses up and took the coffee tray from Loraine's hands, Loraine barely in time to rescue the espresso before it tumbled off. By the time she had it under control, the streetlight blinked DON'T WALK, but Ms. Bartle, staring at the coffee tops in her hands, her glasses slowly sliding down the slope of her nose, had stepped off the curb already.

"Wait, Ms. Bartle," Loraine called after her. Ms. Bartle pushed onward, oblivious to the speeding cars advancing like a mad herd toward her.

"Lord," Loraine muttered as a man in a dark suit dashed into traffic after Ms. Bartle.

A slowing car honked with wild insistence. Ms. Bartle wobbled. A coffee fell over and splattered onto the pavement, making Ms. Bartle wince and bend back to look for stains. The man in the business suit grabbed her elbow and pulled her away from the path of a horn-blaring SUV. He then gently guided them safely across the street, holding his hand out to slow oncoming cars. When the traffic lights had turned again, Loraine hurried to join them. The gentleman had taken the diminished coffee tray from Ms. Bartle.

"Oh dear. I spilled your coffee," Ms. Bartle said to Loraine.

"Thank you," said Loraine, accepting the coffee tray from the man.

"Ma'am, you should be careful," said the man to Ms. Bartle.

"I'm terribly sorry about that coffee, Ms. Loraine," said Ms. Bartle, ignoring him.

Loraine shook her head. She quickly entered the lobby of ABC Vinyl and Siding leaving them both behind. When she got to the office, Ted was standing by Loraine's desk, a hand in his slacks.

"We have a coffee maker in the kitchen," Ted said. "If you want Starbucks, you should get up earlier."

"It's for your client," Loraine argued. She bustled past him into the conference room dispensing coffee to the grateful homeowners. The gesture had been meant to impress Ted. Now she wasn't sure what she had accomplished, and she still had to make her morning quota, calling residential numbers printed on a list, asking them if they'd be willing to meet with one of their consultants, who just happened to be in the area. "Vinyl siding could raise the value of your home at least twenty percent," the speech went. Loraine had it tightly memorized.

It was hours before anyone noticed that Ms. Bartle hadn't come to work. By then, Loraine had told the story of the coffee to the mailman and the UPS guy, then to Luca and to Jose, adding details with every new telling. She acted out Ms. Bartle's look of surprise, waddling comically around.

"Oh, that's so her," Luca said.

People joined in as soon as she began with Latoya, who'd been in the field and hadn't heard it yet.

Afterward, Ariel said, "What's wrong with her?" and Latoya said, "Poor Ms. Bartle," to which Loraine saw fit to add, "Bless her heart."

No one noticed the empty office until it was almost lunchtime.

Luca said, "Guess Ms. Bartle was too embarrassed to show her face today."

"Do you think we should call her?" Loraine proposed, peeling the paper from her dispenser-bought tuna sandwich.

Unlike the other workers, Ms. Bartle didn't have family photos on her desk, only a picture of the Madonna with a rosary hanging from the frame.

Her walls, too, looked bare, except where she'd Scotch-taped a poster of a short prayer over a sundrenched mountain landscape just a tad out of focus. Loraine wondered if the woman had any family. Who would Ted notify if her absence turned out to be something serious?

Her phone buzzed, and Loraine fumbled to fish it out of her purse. It was a text from Jared. *Terry and I would like to go to the Caymans for Christmas. We think Lily would love it.*

Jose elbowed her. "Junero also didn't come in today." He wiggled his eyebrows.

Jose had a theory about everyone. Ariel was gay. Sam had slept with at least two of the senior managers. Latoya in Human Resources was two months' pregnant by Misha from Logistics, "a little bastard kid," Jose called him. To Jose, the office was an ongoing telenovela, the plot twisting with every new episode.

"Weekend honeymoon," she went along with the game.

Loraine texted Jared, *Christmas is my time. We have plans.* She put her sandwich to her nose. It smelled like onion, but the tuna was so old it barely gave off a faint hint of its identity. The edges of the bread had browned and dried.

Jared's response buzzed back within moments. *Lily wants to come with us.*

Loraine tossed the phone into her purse. "I'm going out."

She had meant to make a bank deposit to pay the mortgage but was distracted on the way by clothing shops, already just past Halloween showing Christmas displays, tinfoil, bows and gift-wrapped boxes arranged elegantly in the windows, the perfect picture of a perfect Christmas for whatever perfect family existed in the minds of the store clerks assigned to this task. Loraine scoffed, thinking of her own once-perfect family: married to a man twice her age, just like Mother had wanted her to, a man who had already been married twice, and who barely ever mentioned his first wife. *My first Mrs. Starnes*, he called her, muttering the words into a snifter or speaking them to the burning end of a cigar.

On their second date, Jared told her he'd lost a child in that first marriage. "A tragic death," he'd muttered, wiping his eyes dry with his thumb. The pity story had succeeded in getting her into bed, but after that, he never mentioned the child. Even after they got married, Loraine never saw him visit a gravesite or share a picture of his tragic little girl.

"It hurts too much," he said, if she mentioned it, hiding his prevarications behind a look of grief. Surely he'd made it all up, a ruse by an older man to kindle sympathy from a girl half his age, one he didn't expect to date for much longer than the contract that had taken him temporarily to rural Alabama, where he'd met her. But then she was pregnant with Lily right away, a blessing, yes, but one that locked her into a doomed marriage – she was eighteen, and Christian, and her parents and the community just wouldn't have it any other way. Now, so many years after their divorce, the best thing that had come out of that marriage was still Lily.

Loraine skipped the bank and instead bought a silk blouse she could not afford, intending to wear it for the company party with the tags hidden inside the sleeve so she could return the blouse the next day. She picked up a hot dog at the food court and ate it on the way back to the office, throwing away a bit of bread for each bite of the meat, and still, every window she passed, she looked into it, half expecting to see Ms. Bartle sitting with her purse in her lap.

When she returned to the office, Ms. Bartle sat crouched over her adding machine, the receipt paper curling over the edge of her desk with a gurgle and a buzz.

Ariel looked up and shrugged. "Came in about five minutes ago," he said without breaking the rhythm of his typing. Loraine couldn't explain her relief. The woman was an odd duck, but Loraine worried for her, even as she disliked being around her. Something about Ms. Bartle felt too familiar, too much like what she might have become, had she not had the courage to divorce Jared and raise Lily on her own, regardless of what Mother said.

For the rest of the day, Loraine sat in her office with her finger over the white pages, reading off of a script: "I happen to have an ABC vinyl siding expert in your area. If you want to take advantage of this opportunity, I can offer you a 20 percent discount."

On Saturday, Loraine treated herself and her daughter to a twelve-dollar special mani-pedi at the Korean spa at the mall. They chatted about Lily's college applications to Northwestern and Brown, and Lily's boyfriend being accepted to Pratt in New York, all the while Loraine looking at every customer who stepped in, expecting Ms. Bartle to appear, spying them from behind the glass walls.

"Your daddy wants you for Christmas," Loraine finally announced.

"I know," Lily sighed, somewhat theatrically.

"I suppose I could spend Christmas with your grandmother. We'll go to Ms. Frannie's Christmas potluck. We'll help out at the church."

"Oh, Mom." Lily pursed her lips.

This was unfair, and Loraine knew it, but if she had one fear in the world it was to become old alone, stuck taking care of Mother, two old ladies spending their golden age at church's bingo nights and potluck Wednesdays.

"Really, honey, if you want to go…"

"Terry is such a bore. All she ever talks about are catheters and blood pressure cuffs. Jees, like her night school nursing certificate makes her like Dad or something. Can you imagine two weeks of that? Besides, they want me to share their cabin. Gross?"

Loraine wondered how long this negotiation between Jared and Lily had been going on. Jared had enough money to afford a suite. His job as a hospital administrator ensured solvency, but he was thrifty. From the beginning, they'd argued about money. The master bathroom of their house had a tub painted black and a strobe-like chandelier that embarrassed Loraine enough to shower instead in the guest bathroom. There was a smell of rot and piss coming from the septic tank that oozed out into the living room on rainy days. Jared had gone out to the backyard, dug up the septic, puttered down there with long boots and wrenches, then turned in declaring victory, but the smell never went away, and when Loraine hired a plumber to clean it out, Jared held up the bill like it was murder evidence. He divided the total by six; then he reduced that amount from her monthly grocery allowance. For the next six months, Loraine had cut up food coupons and served him Kroger brand mac and cheese.

"Might be a good way to spend some time with your dad," she told Lily.

With her peripheral vision, she thought she saw a woman in a gray dress duck into a Victoria's Secret shop. Ms. Bartle? The name seared her skin. A crowd of people passed, obscuring her view, and when they left, there was no Ms. Bartle, only a woman in a gray suit with a similar body shape.

Lily released a tragic sigh. "I don't have to go. Not if you're going to be miserable."

"Well, how about you and I go somewhere fun together this year? Just you and I?"

"Can we go to California?"

Loraine didn't think she could afford California, considering Lily's choices of college applications, but Lily sang, "Malibu beach, here we come."

"We'd have to share a room," Loraine warned. "I don't have your father's salary."

Lily sank back into the massage chair, humming "California Dreaming."

Loraine let it go. Monday she might tell her daughter that California wasn't an option, but for now, she didn't want to spoil the mood, all light and joy, a sunny weekend of chirping birds and bargain sales.

By the time Monday rolled around, Loraine had all but forgotten Ms. Bartle, which is why she was startled when the woman skulked behind her on the MARTA platform. Ms. Bartle was wearing vampire red shoes and a drab gray skirt suit, which she'd attempted to liven up with a cherry-red scarf.

Loraine tried to decode what she felt, a static discomfort that seemed a harbinger of a bad week to come. Fate had conspired for this meeting to occur in the rumble of oncoming and departing trains.

"Ms. Bartle," she snapped.

Ms. Bartle pursed her lips. Her lipstick, Loraine noticed, was of a shade of adolescent pink unsuited to a woman her age.

"Ms. Bartle, everywhere I go, there you are. Are you following me?"

"Oh dear," Ms. Bartle said. "I'm afraid I'm simply not good at this kind of thing anymore." She threw her cherry-red scarf over her shoulder. She then extended her hand as if to shake and make up, but she leaned into it, her mouth stretched into a grimace that looked more painful than welcoming.

Loraine found she had an urge to propel herself away from this woman, up the stairs toward the honking cars and busy pedestrians.

"You really don't know about me, do you?" Ms. Bartle said.

What an odd thing to say: they had worked in the same office for months now, but true, she really didn't know Ms. Bartle beyond that aloof and slightly odd behavior that prompted any normal person to feel uncomfortable in her presence.

Ms. Bartle looked like she was trying to smile while also trying to hold back something so spiny and bitter that it twisted her mouth in a deformed grimace. "So he never told you about me? I thought… You seem to like the talk."

Loraine instinctively stepped back. "Ted keeps his employees' lives private," she said.

She did not want to have a conversation about Ms. Bartle here, in this place, and be corralled into offering apologies, or expressing the type of false sympathies her Mother was so fond of dispensing at church.

Another train rumbled past. Ms. Bartle spoke again, but the loud ding of the station speakers and the announcement of the incoming train drowned out her words. A herd of people, pressed together shoulder to shoulder, stepped onto the platform in a strange rhythm of purposeful footsteps, each beating at the pace of a cosmic clock that Loraine, too, could feel ticking under her skin.

Part of her wanted to stay, to listen to Ms. Bartle's story, whatever it was that had turned her so quietly peculiar, and yet there was also a pulsing of fear inside her, a sense that something weighty and burdensome would fall on her lap from Ms. Bartle's mouth, something she would not want to carry with her out of the station, across the street and into the office.

Loraine turned away from her and into the crowd. It felt protective at first, the impatient jostles beckoning her to keep up to the march, people buffering all sides like a phalanx. She held a hand to her heart. Someone's briefcase scratched against her calf, putting a run in her pantyhose. A woman bumped into her purse. Loraine didn't quite seem to be able to keep up. She stepped onto the escalator and looked down at Ms. Bartle, so very still on that platform, her mouth now reassembled in a faint grin, that hideous lipstick making her stand out in the crowd.

At first Loraine told no one about the odd encounter, still shaking from the irrational fear that Ms. Bartle's pitiable misery was going to rub off on her. She studiously avoided Bartle's cubicle for as long as she could keep herself at her desk. By eleven, she broke down and found Ariel at his desk.

"Ms. Bartle is stalking me," she said. "Every day I see that crazy woman's face everywhere I go."

Ariel sighed and swiveled around toward Bartle's empty cubicle. "She works here." He went on typing, and Loraine couldn't help but think of Ms. Bartle, watching her walk away from that train platform.

Sam gave Loraine more ear time in the lady's room. She widened her eyes at all the right pauses. "Hideous," she said about Ms. Bartle's new outfit. "Just ignore her," she said. "Everyone else does."

At lunch, Jose said, "What are you gonna do? It's not like you can take out a restraining order. She works here."

"I want her to stop following me."

"Go tell her. While you're at it, lend her some lipstick."

"Do you think she's dangerous?"

Jose shrugged. "That scarf could give you glaucoma."

When Loraine returned to her desk, she was just in time to see Ms. Bartle scuttle away around the corner, clutching something to her chest. Loraine was distracted by the buzz of her cellphone: a voicemail message from Jared. *The length you will go to distance me from Lily! Last year you sued me for more child support, and now you've got enough to vacation in Hollywood? Terry and I have been planning our cruise for months.*

Her ex's self-important, booming voice was sauce for her barbecued nerves. Loraine redialed Jared's number. "You had her last year," she snapped to his voicemail. "This Christmas is mine." She grabbed for something on her desk out of habit, but her fingers grasped at nothing. She felt the object missing before she knew what she was looking for. The phone buzzed back almost immediately. She didn't look at the text message. Instead she focused on her desk to remember what was missing. And then she realized what it was, a personalized "Best Mom" mug with hers and Lily's picture on it that Lily had gifted her on Mother's Day. Loraine saw the faintly shaped mark framing the circle where the mug had been.

The unread text message from Jared dinged again on her phone.

She did a mental inventory of her things, her paperweight, her stapler, her Lucite nameplate; she opened her desk drawer and slammed it shut. Her cell dinged again. Something else was gone, a picture, one of Lily that she'd taken on a beach on Tybee Island and pinned to the corkboard behind her computer. It was gone.

The thought of Ms. Bartle collecting her daughter's photos gave her pause.

Mother always said, "The world is full of crazy people." What did Ms. Bartle want with her? Had she been stalking Lily, too? Maybe she really had seen Ms. Bartle at the mall, not a woman who looked like her. Loraine's hands shook as she speed-dialed her daughter's number.

"Mom?"

"Honey, are you okay?"

"Yeah, why?"

Ted knocked on her office door. He was holding a manila folder she guessed to be the new brick and veneer renovation price schedules.

"Lily, sweetie, I want you to stay near one of your teachers until I come and get you today, okay?"

Lily didn't respond.

"Did you hear me?"

"What happened?"

"Nothing. Nothing happened. Just do as I say, okay, honey?"

"You're scaring me, Mom."

Ted leaned in, mouthed, "You okay?"

"I love you, sweetie," she said into the phone, and hung up.

"What's going on?"

"Bartle, your *poor Ms. Bartle*. She follows me around like a stray, like she wants to be adopted and then she snuck in here and stole my mug."

"Your mug?" Ted's face looked disingenuously dumb. "We have mugs..."

"It had a picture of Lily." Loraine rose, and her chair rolled back, hitting the wall. "And she stole another picture. What does she want with my daughter?"

Ted closed the door behind him.

"I'm telling you. She's been stalking me for days. I saw her. I saw her near my desk just now. She has no business here."

"You say she broke into your office to steal your mug and a picture?"

"Don't." Her pen pointed to his chest. "I just saw her."

Ted lifted his palm, a pen still hanging between his fingers. "She's been working here for, what, twenty years? For god's sake, Loraine, try to get along."

Loraine made to go for the door. Ted stepped in front of her. "Look, she's a little strange, I'll admit, but she's a fragile woman."

"Fragile how?" Loraine snapped. "Fragile enough to show up at my house with a butcher knife one day? I don't care if she was kidnapped by ISIS terrorists. That freak gets near my daughter and I'm calling the police."

Ted's face took on a hardness that made her think of Jared. "You probably put that picture someplace you don't remember." The way he spoke reminded her of Jared all those nights he came home smelling of whiskey and smoke, telling her, it's such a boring thing, a woman's jealousy.

When she stepped out into the hall, Sam looked up from her desk. Jose was standing by the photocopying machine, a sheaf of papers in his hands, his tie loosened.

"What's going on?"

"Nothing," Ted said. "Get back to work."

"Ms. Bartle and I are gonna have a word," Loraine said, marching, fist clenched to her office cubicle. The chair was empty. Her purse was gone. Loraine tried to open a drawer in her desk. It was locked.

"Don't do that," said Ted. "You have no right to do that."

Loraine opened another drawer, pushed aside a stapler, broken pens, an open box of paperclips. She searched deep in the drawer. Business cards. Prescription pills. She pulled them out. Lithium Carbonate. "Well, hell." She shook the bottle at Ted's face. "Isn't that dandy."

"Don't make me call security."

Loraine reached farther back into the drawer and felt the edges of a large manila envelope tucked so far in that it had fallen behind the drawer, with only the red string and flap hung high enough for her to feel with the tips of her fingers. As she pulled, the envelope caught against the angles of the drawer and ripped a little. Loraine gave it a sharp tug and it came loose. The bottom end was fat with something, photos in glossy three-by-fives. They stuck together as Loraine peeled them apart. The ones at the bottom of the envelopes looked old and grayish green.

Loraine didn't recognize any of the people in the pictures. "There," she kept saying. "There," expecting Lily's face, or her own, to emerge from the grimed, fingerprinted surface of the old glossies. But the only face she recognized was that of a much younger Ms. Bartle, her arms draped over the shoulders of a pretty child, maybe two years old, wide brow, dark eyes, hair twisted in auburn corkscrew curls like Lily's, a child with a head that seemed far too large for someone her age. Loraine was about to make a connection between this child and Ms. Bartle, a breath-stunting realization, when Ted pulled the photograph from her hands.

"Loraine," he said, nostrils flaring. "Take the rest of the day."

Hydrocephalus is what Jared had called it, fluid accumulating in the brain, making a child's head grow larger than normal. For seconds at a time, Loraine wasn't sure if the buzzing she heard came from the overhead lights or her own head. The photocopying machine's fan hummed rhythmically under the beat of Ted's now agitated voice, his words never shaping into meaning in her mind.

When she got up her knees gave. She held onto Ms. Bartle's desk. She wobbled to the ladies' bathroom, hearing Ted behind her sighing out his fatherly, "Loraine." The bathroom was locked, of course. She spoke to the door: "Ms. Bartle? This ain't how we do things around here. Come on out."

The toilet flushed, and Loraine waited, but the door didn't open.

Loraine knocked. "You plan on hiding in there all day?"

The sink faucet turned on, then off. The garbage lid clanged into place.

"Ms. Bartle? We have to talk. Now."

Loraine knocked while Ted's voice rose by degrees. "This behavior among employees..." Ariel and Jose and LaToya crowded behind them. Loraine knocked. "Ms. Bartle?"

The faucet turned off. The toilet flushed.

The bathroom door clicked open. Ms. Bartle's eyes, dull and wet, looked like cracked candy. She held Lily's picture to her breast, the photo folded in four, probably creased with white lines already. Her lipstick bled into the corner of her mouth. They looked at each other for a breath, maybe two, but Loraine knew what was coming. She felt it like some people feel rain, like a cold whisper in the bones. Ms. Bartle cried out what sounded like a cat's howl, but Loraine understood. She heard the words in it, "My child, just like your Lily..."

Shame split Loraine from her chest up to her skull. She saw herself waddling around the office, imitating Ms. Bartle's wobble, mocking the old lady, and Ms. Bartle, folding into shadows in crowded shopping malls, whispering into the noise of traffic, Ms. Bartle stepping out of a train, or waiting at a window booth, Ms. Bartle running after the shadow of her child, collecting pieces of the dead through the dusty mementos and discarded conversations of other women's lives.

Ms. Bartle shook with a sob.

"Now, Ms. Bartle," Jose said. "You can't just go and take other people's stuff."

Ted said, "Ms. Bartle. We're going to have a talk in my office."

But Loraine had already folded Beatrice into her arms, owning the woman's sobbing. Her heavy round body hiccupped hard against her chest, getting her blouse wet. Loraine rubbed circles on her back, whispering, "You'll come over tonight to meet her. We'll show you all her pictures. There, there, now, Ms. B. There, there."

MURDER BY GHOST

At three in the morning, Lindsey was still awake, the digital recorder whirring tirelessly on the windowsill. Jessie had brought it over after school, and she'd sworn that if Lindsey let it play all night, it would pick up the voices of ghosts, but Daddy had ruined it coming home, with the usual jingle of keys hitting the kitchen counter, long sighs as his shoes dropped, cabinets opened and shut. Lindsey shifted under the covers, tracking Daddy's movements from the hall to the kitchen to the mudroom and back into the kitchen. She turned off the recorder, but for a moment or two she stared at the circles forming on the ceiling from the streetlights. For the time it took for a headlight's reflection to cross the room and vanish, she imagined – almost wished – that the sounds downstairs were those of an intruder. A burglar. A murderer. She squashed that wish with the pillows she now pressed against her ears to shush the noises from downstairs.

Lindsey could tell that Daddy was drunk again, but, at least, he wasn't calling out to her in that urgent voice, *Lindsaaahhhy*, until she hurried downstairs and found him wobbling in the kitchen, his eyes bobbing and unfocused, rubber fingers barely able to hang onto the whiskey glass. He'd have something boiling on the stove, or heating in the microwave.

"Did you eat yet?"

"Yes, Daddy. It's really late."

"Is it?"

He'd check the cat-face clock behind the wall first, then his iPhone, everything he did predictable, like the stages of a virus.

Sometimes, if she didn't go downstairs after he called her, she'd find him in the morning, sleeping on his feet, elbows on counter, face on hands, a half-eaten sandwich laying on the cutting board next to a head of lettuce, a sliced tomato, and a package of ham, all of which she'd throw directly into the trash.

Tonight, though she did hear him open the freezer and tinker with ice-cubes, at least he wasn't making his usual grunting noises and dropping things (a fork, a plastic container, a glass or plate, or jar of pickles—the evidence shattered and scattered over the floor for her to clean up in the morning).

Lindsey made an effort and moved the comforter aside, her feet touching the carpet. Daddy's routine had been pretty much the same since cancer took Mama. These days, Lindsey held her breath and tiptoed carefully around her Daddy. Mama was gone, but something had gotten into Daddy. It wasn't cancer, but it ate at him all the same.

"Daddy? Is that you?" she called from the top of the stairs. A square of oily light spilled onto the carpet from the kitchen.

Her daddy appeared at the kitchen's entrance, hovering just a step behind the square of light. His eyes were dull and heightened by dark circles. His hair had grown too long, and curled around the ears.

"Sweetheart. What are you doing up? It's late, darling."

It was such a relief to hear him talk without a slur that she thought about fixing him that plate he was probably fixing for himself.

"I just wanted to tell you that tomorrow night I won't be home for dinner. I'm going out with friends, okay? I might be late."

Her daddy leaned against the wall. "Is everything okay?"

"Sure. Why?"

"Just want to make sure, that's all. You're going out with some friends, huh?"

"We're going ghost hunting, some stupid thing that Jessie wants to do."

He waved his hand. "You go on ahead and have a good time. Catch me a big ghost, okay, darling?"

"Sure, Daddy."

He whistled the Ghostbusters tune.

Jessie had been obsessed with ghosts since she was little, but Lindsey didn't believe in an afterlife. Mommy had been Catholic, but Daddy was Jewish, and at school everyone was pretty much either Baptist or Presbyterian, which either way seemed to exclude her from the circle of self-proclaimed good Christians except when someone from school, inspired by the pastor or by the promise of heavenly reward, stopped by way too early on a Sunday morning and invited her to church.

Sometimes, she'd go. It was all a big deal of hand clapping and singing. If she could have stepped out of the cage of her grief for even just a breath, she would have probably appreciated it. Mommy always used to say that God was a celebration, that the only true prayer was a prayer of joy. It would seem possible that the singing and the *amens* and the preacher's *hallelujahs* were a celebration, a unified shout of joy to God, but in the trappings of mourning, the exhilaration of believers swaying and holding hands felt like a travesty. Lindsey did not—could not—bring herself to believe their hearts were lifted by anything other than the lie that was the music.

Miss Greenfield, the science teacher, described that ecstasy as a biological process, a momentary slowing of the frontal lobe activity in the brain, an effect that enabled one to feel like a child, and to enjoy intense sensory stimuli. A neurochemical illusion, in other words.

Before Mommy died, Lindsey would have preferred to think of life as a celebration, but watching her mother drained of life and spirit day by day had hardened her inside. In the end, what smiled at her behind the skull-like face was not her Mommy, but sickness itself.

Lindsey remembered having gone home after the funeral, looking at things and not recognizing them. The trees were not trees, but specters trapped in the cement. The draping Spanish moss, hanging from high limbs, was life itself giving up, peeling away from the world like rotted bark. And people hadn't seemed like people either; just walking ghosts, clinging to delusions channeled through smartphone and HD television.

"I don't want to talk to ghosts," she told Jessie.

"But don't you want to know?"

"Know what? People die, and they're gone. Let it be, Jessie, okay?"

But lately Jessie had been on a mission. She'd bought her own equipment, something she called a spirit box, and an EMF recorder. Once she'd forced Lindsey to listen to her digital recorder for nearly an hour for what sounded like static with the occasional faint echo of people talking from far away.

"Did you hear that?" Jessie leaned in on the recorder, her breath smelling like her strawberry granola bar, nibbled and forgotten in her lap in a nest of crumbs and torn foil. Jessie played it again. There was a slight interruption in the static, and sure, Lindsey could hear the voice of someone talking casually, but certainly not a ghost.

"She said, help me," Jessie cried, bouncing on her knees on the bed.

"For God's sake, she did not."

"She did, too. Listen."

All Lindsey heard on the replay was static, and yes, a faint female voice emerged from the surf of white noise, but what she said was too distant to make out. It was like listening to a long-distance phone call when the satellite signal got crossed.

"If it's a voice, it's probably something you picked up from the local radio, or maybe even just a person down the street."

"You get so critical, sometime," Jessie said. She sighed, her chest rising and falling. "I didn't want to say anything, but even Chuck says it. It's like you hate everybody and everything."

"Chuck." She rolled her eyes, though she had to admit it hurt to picture the two of them discussing her... where? Between classes? By the lockers? Without her?

Chuck wasn't the cutest kid in school, but he wore shirts that said, "May The Forest Be With You" and "I'm not Roundup Ready," and if anyone mentioned the weather, he'd rake his hand through that mop of jet-black hair that fell over half his face, and get on a mission, quoting things he'd read about fire coming out of people's kitchen faucets. Once, Sid Landon in Chemistry had called him a tampon-face in Miss Greenfield's class, and with the smoothest baritone, and in under five minutes' time, Chuck explained the consequences of Climate Change and the risks of ignoring it, concluding with "Blood Breath" to counter Sid's "Tampon Face." The other kids were so taken aback that they applauded. Chuck stood up and took a bow.

So, she was *negative*. What did that even mean? An inverted charge carried by an electron, or a value less than zero. *Don't be so negative, sweetheart. A kid like you should be psyched to be alive.*

"It's like you don't even care about us. Do you even notice us?"

"Of course, I care." Lindsey stood up. "It's just that if you died I'd hope that you stayed dead." She hadn't meant it the way it came out, but all the same she left Jessie sitting on her bed and headed downstairs and into the kitchen. She slammed cabinet doors shut and clinked plates together, the source of her hurt scurrying inside her like a frightened mouse.

The blender was half full of an unrecognizable pinkish sludge that looked like it had congealed overnight. The vodka bottle sat in a puddle of that sludge, with Daddy's half-drained glass serving as a watering hole for a swarm of fruit flies.

Jessie had followed her down. "What are you doing?"

Lindsey was embarrassed by the half-eaten sandwich, the glass, the sludge in the blender, splatters of pink on the counter and cabinets, and a sliced onion browning on the cutting board. She didn't want Jessie to see it, but Jessie looked around, something in her expression making her suddenly seem older.

"Let's get this cleaned up," she said. She moved like she'd waited in bars for years. She emptied the pink mix drink in the sink and wiped the counter with paper towels.

Lindsey picked up the bottle of vodka and smelled it. She'd smelled vodka before, of course. She'd had drinks with her friends at parties, but Daddy's vodka smelled different, an odor like a sanitized hospital room, with something else oozing underneath, faintly pungent and earthy, something that she associated with Daddy's sloppy kisses on her forehead, his weeping, "I love you so much, you know that, don't you?"

Jessie was tying up the trash bag when she said, "Chuck said he'd come. He asked about you. He wanted to know how you were."

"You lie."

Jessie went on to haul the trash to the garage, her pink hair over her face veiling her smile.

Out of all the ghost attractions, the group that Jessie had put together settled on the Gribble House, an abandoned warehouse made famous by a reality show. In the 1890s a triple ax murder had taken place in a house that stood where now there was only the warehouse. The tour company had a fancy website with clips from the show and historical information on the murders. Lindsey felt a little nauseated reading some of the testimonies, phrases people thought they'd heard. Reading it took her back to her Mama on the wheelchair, Mama losing muscle and color, fading with the yellow of the couch downstairs, her voice calm as she told Lindsey how to arrange the pillow behind her head, then to get Daddy for the catheter and after, to take the clothes out of the dryer, *okay, honey?*— as if it were just a normal day, dying another chore to check off the digital notepad on the refrigerator.

Lindsey almost didn't go, but Chuck showed up at the door, his truck parked in the driveway. Chuck, as Jessie had promised. The long sweep of hair that usually covered his right eye in school was slicked back with gel, tonight, and the hair around his ears was buzzed close to his scalp.

"Hey," he said when he saw her, his teeth flashing briefly as his hand went up.

"You got a haircut."

He shrugged. "Needed a job."

She sat shotgun in his truck. "Hey." He kept his head low, looking into his hands. "Sorry about, you know…"

"Please, change the subject," she said.

"What subject." Jessie slid into the back seat. "Is it about ghosts?"

"I like ghosts," Chuck said. "This was a cool idea."

"It's Jessie's thing," Lindsey said quickly, and then she was sorry she did because, as his hand reached for the ignition, Chuck looked into the rearview making eye contact with Jessie. A smile crept on his face. She told herself to stay positive, whatever that meant, but her belly pulsed with a hot, nagging feeling.

Downtown was alive with horse carriages and tourists on beer-walking tours. Jessie, Chuck, and Lindsey piled out of the truck and met the ghost guide at the gate of the warehouse, where Jessie's cousins and a couple of kids from school were waiting. Tracy was a tall, skinny man, with thickly rimmed glasses and long hair, which he'd gathered up in a bun that looked premeditatedly messy. He spoke with a loud pitch to his voice as though he were trying to sell them something, though they'd already paid their discounted student tickets. He gave them equipment similar to what Jessie had shown Lindsey in her bedroom, a static noise maker that he called a Spirit Box, and an EMF recorder, and some other thing that was supposed to turn red if a ghost touched it, which Terry called a pod. Chuck surprised everyone by bringing his own set.

"You like doing ghost things?" Lindsey asked when she saw him unfold it out of a sheet of black velvety fabric.

"Been doing it for years," he said. "That's why I got a haircut and a job. Ghost hunting can get expensive. Someday, I'll show you some of the cool things I caught on camera."

Lindsey followed Tracy into the warehouse. They walked around in the dark. It was one of those hot, muggy Savannah summer nights, and being in an unventilated warehouse made it worse. Lindsey was sweating through her tank top, her ponytail sticking to the back of her neck. She kept wiping her neck with a paper tissue, looking for Chuck who had leaped on ahead, trying to look like she was not looking for Chuck, then bashing herself mentally when she did see him, wholly engrossed with Tracy's nerd talk on the technical aspects of their ghost equipment. As they walked, she felt a puff of cool air on her neck, which made Jessie squeak, "Did you feel that?"

"No." She lied rather than getting into it, part of her "staying positive" plan.

Was there something wrong with her that she couldn't buy into this scam? A business of this kind could easily rig some equipment to make a chill puff of air go off at intervals in different areas of the warehouse. But Chuck and Jessie were all over it, *oohing* and *aahing* with eyes wide, and texting posts, Tweeting the speed of their blinking red lights. The more they roamed, the more Lindsey felt like she was the ghost, unable to connect with her school friends except with a cold touch, a breath of jumbled words whispered under a lot of static.

Chuck came up behind her. "I have to show you something," he whispered into her neck. He was so close his long strand of hair tickled her cheek. He led her by the elbow, distancing them from the group and heading to the area that Terry called the slave quarters. "It's awesome. Check it out," he said. And then he was no longer beside her but hovering over a tripod set up to face a few chairs in a semicircle, which she vaguely remembered Terry having said was a REM pod. Chuck leaned over it, wholly absorbed with its functions and buttons.

A scruffy-looking Raggedy Ann doll sat on the chair opposite the pod. Lindsey could hear the excited squeaks of the other kids from the other rooms as they compared each other's impressions of this blipping red thing or that static-sounding something-or-other.

"What's this doll doing here?" she asked.

Chuck kept tinkering with the REM pod. "Hold on. Almost done."

Lindsey sat next to the doll.

"Don't touch that doll yet," he warned.

She drew her hand away. It was a cheap thing, legs stiff with sawdust and fabric, eyes and lips painted on the flat, plastic surface of her face. Only her dress had some cuteness to it, red, ruffled, and short. But her frozen face, perpetually smiling, though barely visible in the red glow of the pod lights, seemed too close a metaphor for the way she felt about herself.

"Kind of clichéd, don't you think? Ghosts and toys? Next, they'll just push a clown this way, and the show will be complete."

Chuck gave her an absentminded, "Hold on. I'll show you something awesome."

But too late. Already Lindsey couldn't get out of her mind the last days Mama spent at home, on that couch downstairs because she could no longer make it upstairs, the smell of the microwave dinners for her and Daddy because Mama really couldn't hold down her food anymore, the cardboard boxes piled up in the trash. Lindsey felt that cool shiver of air that had made Jessie squeak. The REM pod winked its red eye once.

"Woah!" Chuck said. "Did you just touch the doll?"

"The doll?"

"That's what I wanted to show you. Touch it now. The ghosts go crazy."

The thought that something not quite dead might still be here, clinging to that piece of rag and sawdust, filled her with a nebulous gray dread.

She wanted to go home. She scraped back the chair and got up, and saw that weird grin spreading over Chuck's face, his brown eyes getting large with excitement, and she felt like throwing up. She almost belched. She put a hand to her mouth.

Tracy emerged into the glow of the pod. "You're not supposed to leave the group." He gave them both an oblique look. "Chuck, my man, you got a REM pod setup? Talk to me."

"Just look at the temperature. Jessie touched the doll."

"Lindsey. I'm Lindsey. I touched the doll."

Chuck narrowed his eyes on his laser thermometer. Terry went to the doll and touched it. Something about his self-importance set her off.

"Death is good business for you, isn't it? What do you care that people died here, what their family might think of all this show? Ka-ching, right?"

"Hey, we bought the ticket," Chuck said.

"You kids shouldn't be here alone," Tracy said. "Shouldn't mess with the ghosts. It can get to be a problem."

"You think they messed with us?" Chucked moved toward her and touched her forehead the way her daddy did. "She's cold."

She winced and slapped Chuck's hand away. She hadn't meant to, but somehow doing it made her want to do it again. That gray feeling inside her had built up, and Chuck was so close to her, his beautiful slick hair over his beautiful, soulful eyes, and yet he said, "Could they actually have got into her, you think?"

Chuck: another living zombie. How stupid of her to have missed it. Chuck, dumb like everyone else, asleep while awake, going through the motions of school and soccer, homework and parties, without seeing how death pressed against the brittle barriers they had all erected around their routine, their plans for college, their D&D parties, their texting and gaming and dating, all of it a toxic poison oozing slowly through the permeable membranes of their make-believe world.

"Interesting," Tracy said. The REM pod winked its red eye rapidly, maybe sixteen times. Chuck and Tracy shared a look, wonder passing between them.

"Is this a joke?" Lindsey heard how strident her voice sounded. She snatched the doll and shook it. "It's just a stupid doll."

"Hey, careful with that," Tracy said. He tried to get the doll from her but she stepped away, holding the doll up by its brittle arm.

"Put it down, Lindsey. The ghosts are going crazy," Chuck said.

"There are no ghosts. The dead are gone, Chuck. The heart stops beating, and that's it, you're gone."

The REM blinked several red flashes, drawing a gasp from both Terry and Chuck, and Lindsey, Lindsey couldn't say what was going through her, but something, sawing and cold, and real, like sickness, like drunk smells, and hunger, and rot.

"You'd better put that doll down," Terry said, his hand on her elbow, so serious and full of himself she couldn't help but make fun of him.

"Put the doll down, Lindsey," she mocked.

"That thing is not a toy," Terry said.

"Really?" A tinny, hysterical laughter came out of her. The doll. That thing that smiled at her with a dumb, unchanging expression. Terry lunged for it and she pulled back, then angry, without thinking, she hit him with it. He held up his arms, crying, "Hey!"

"Hey!" she cried back, hitting him again, and again, the doll making a dull thud against his arms and elbows. "Hey! Hey!"

"Ouch. What the hell? Stop."

Lindsey couldn't stop. She was telling herself to but her arm kept slamming the doll against Terry's stupid head. Chuck rushed over, made a grab for it but when she tugged it back, a stitch popped open and sawdust bled onto the cement. She dropped the doll then, but when Terry tried to retrieve it, she jumped on it with both feet.

"There," she said, dizzy and oddly satisfied.

"Why the fuck did you just do that?" Chuck's voice came out strangled.

Terry knelt over the doll like over a murder victim.

"Now they'll really be mad, huh?" she said. "Watch out. Murder by ghost."

Chuck looked unreal in the blinking red light, dumb like the doll. Some of the kids in the other room had trickled in, grins plastered on their faces. Someone said, "Did you see her whaling on that guy?" The other kid pumped fists. "Best ghost hunt *ever.*"

Lindsey pushed past them and ran through the long warehouse. She ran outside. The minute her shoes hit the front steps, the Savannah heat devoured her, clinging to her clothes and skin like hot breath.

"Oh shit!" She held her hand to her mouth in a convulsion of sobs. "Oh shit."

Moments later, the warehouse door opened. Jessie stepped out from behind the heavy front door. "Are you all right? What happened?"

"Oh my God, Lindsey. My mama's dead." The words slid out of her mouth in a slur. "Mama's dead, and she's killing my daddy."

It was three in the morning when the taxi dropped her off. Lindsey could still see the light on in the kitchen inside. She went in.

"Daddy?" she called out. The stairway light was on, but the upstairs was dark. Lindsey slammed the front door behind her and peered into the darkened living room. The TV was off, and the pillows on the couch looked untouched. Only an empty glass on the coffee table suggested there had been anyone at all.

Lindsey picked up the glass and went into the kitchen. She could hear Daddy's snores, but she didn't see him at first. She found him on the floor behind the island, naked, cross-legged, asleep, a broken plate of spaghetti toppled in front of him, sauce and noodles stuck to the floor. His chin touched his chest. He looked like a Buddhist penitent, meditating on impermanence.

She took the scoop and swept up the broken plate and the spaghetti. Then with a wad of wet paper towels, she mopped up the dirt on the floor. She didn't wake Daddy: if she shook him a little, he might look up with a startled gasp, stare at her with eyes, empty of sense, and after a moment, he'd put on a smile and cry, "Hi, sweetheart!" He'd still be dreaming.

Instead, she went upstairs and slipped off her shoes. She climbed on top of the bed with her clothes on. If she were dust, she'd climb on a wind wave and ride it off to a desert. If she were a beam of light, she'd break apart through a glass pane and turn into colors: in a year she'd be so far away that the earth behind her would be a gray pixel in a black sky. Unrecognizable. Invisible. Gone forever and for good.

PRESCRIPTIONS FOR LIFE

We have a prescription for anything that ails you. This one is standard. Take it once a day, every day, before breakfast. Get on a regimen. You'll notice within a month or two, no more migraines. It may cause nausea, and it may alter your moods. In a few studies, subjects reported hair growth on the nipple area. The nausea should go away after a week, but you'll want to do something about your moods.

Take this pill three times a day before every meal, but after you've had something to eat. You might notice a slight weight gain. Increase your exercise routine and stay off carbs and fats. Don't eat any fruit. Keep your protein intake to less than six ounces a day, and you'll be fine. In case you start noticing blood in your stool, a rare side effect, take this every night before bedtime. There may be an increased frequency in your urination, and moderate-to-severe stomach cramps.

Those effects should wear out within the first two weeks, but if that were not the case, we have a prescription you'll love. It has a slight euphoric effect, but it's a magnificent anti-inflammatory. Of course, in rare cases, it causes cysts and kidney failure, but we proactively counteract that with this one, a doozy. Just approved by the FDA. I had the rep here in my office not an hour ago. We're all very excited about it. Take it once a week for three weeks only. It's addictive, that's why we'll have you come back in three weeks and monitor you for signs of paranoia, but as far as pain mitigation goes? It's the best, and there are nearly no side effects.

Some people reported auditory hallucinations, but if you start feeling strange, or if your family members tell you that you're acting strange, here is a number to call. It's 24/7. In less than one percent of cases, people jump out of windows, but if you should get the urge, call the number.

Just for precaution, take this, too. Two hours before lunch, and once at bedtime, but if you take it together with the migraine medicine, then wait an hour, do a headstand – it increases the blood flow to your head. Make sure you have something on your stomach, but not a full meal, and don't ever mix it with pills you take for nausea. Don't drive for two hours after ingestion, and don't operate heavy machinery. If you notice black spots in your vision, increase your dose and cut your protein intake.

It's not complicated. You'll get used to it. Depressing? No, no. This blue little pill right here will make you feel like you're floating above clouds, dancing with fires. You won't even know you're alive. Aren't you feeling anything yet?

LOGORRHEA

The obstetrician was the first to notice. She held the head of the baby, asking the mother for one last push. Words slipped out of the birth canal attached to the baby's skin along with caul and amniotic fluid. The nurse held the baby up to the light to be sure, and the look in the physician's eyes confirmed it. Words. One-syllables at first, sluggish as they dripped from the baby's belly button, even after the umbilical cord was cut and secured; thin, transparent, and as liquid as spit. After only a few seconds of exposure to the sanitized air, the words dried up from the pink knot on the baby's belly and took on a consistency like cotton, adhering stubbornly to the baby's wet skin as if they'd had as much to do with her birth as biology and evolution.

Though the words were in no language either the doctor or the nurse could recognize, they both felt it was unnecessary to worry the parents, nor to make waste of such absorbent matter as these stretchy, gauze-like words that seemed to string together in plush, nonsensical fluff around the baby's fatty legs, lulling the innocent thing into a deep and comfortable sleep. And there was the baby, washed clean of placenta, red still from the effort of breathing, her cheeks pink, her hands little fists, and her feet kicking at the threads of syllables which spun gently around her tiny toes, vowels growing as if encouraged by the baby's mewls into wispy, soft tufts, so that the baby's skin was swathed in a colorless fuzz. The mother held the phrase-trussed baby to her breast. The baby looked into her mother's eyes, opened her pink mouth and a word slid with her drool from the corner of her lip to her chin. It dried, and floated up with the waft of a fan on the tip of her mother's nose, its width no larger than a cat's hair. This made the baby smile.

"Sweet," said the mother.

The father took a picture.

In the months to come the words, which up to then had remained a neutral color like saliva, began to gain consistency similar to the filaments of a spider web, tiny tendrils, nearly transparent, but capable of capturing both light and sound, and of trapping within their secret geometries fragmented descriptions of the baby's observations. Here was a cylinder the color of tap water, the mother's curve of a wrist as she washed the neck of a faucet, her mother's voice hovering over the note of a song she had already forgotten. The words still mostly made no sense, but the parents had soon forgotten to try to decode them, busy changing the soiled diapers and the drooled-on bibs, and in preparing mushy vegetable pastes with their new juicer so that the baby could digest organic food. Now and again the baby would get Mother excited by smacking her lips together as she blew out her vowels, sounding a little like *mahmahmahmah*, but the real words, which had now turned from an indecipherable language to Sanskrit and Esperanto, eluded the baby yet, dancing just beyond the grasp of her little fists, scurrying up her chest and under her chin with the dribble of food that her tongue could not lap up.

Then, the baby grew up. The mother was embarrassed to talk about the words. If at first the manifestation of phrases had been an interesting curiosity, a baby with wispy locks of words curling on the fontanel with her blonde hair, now as a toddler, the words grew into complete sentences out of interpretations of the baby's daily interaction with television. There was the occasional f-word changing from verb to noun to adjective when the toddler had accidentally overheard the soundtrack of a gangster film, and there was no dressing up of pink onesies, bibs, and baby hat that could keep the clever rhythms of the f-haikus from spontaneously forming on the baby's fatty rolls. Moreover, the words were no longer so much like fabric, but like tiny tattoos that appeared mysteriously on the toddler's skin along with scratches and scabs and diaper rashes.

When the child began to sleep in her own bed, she dreamed of being surrounded by a circle of adult dream-ghosts who taunted her by asking simple questions, for which she had no voice to answer. "What is your name?" the dream-people asked. "Where are your parents? Where do you go to school?" She would open her mouth and let out only a strained hiss, while the dream-people, standing akimbo in a circle around her, would glower and frown and repeat their questions, until the child woke up screaming, the words bouncing gleefully from wall to wall of her bedroom, turning into yellow ducks and blue elephants before fluttering back down to her flesh and imprinting themselves in minuscule polka dots on her skin.

It seemed to the child that the words had turned stubborn, guided by a tantalizing sort of magic that rested just beyond her grasp, similar to that which made toys come alive as soon as she fell asleep, reverting to a mocking stillness the very second she opened her eyes. But if she'd never witnessed toys moving of their own volition, at least the words had played with her alphabet soup, matching in cereal texture and color whatever random combination of letters appeared on the oily surface of her chicken broth. Still, in a cruel reversal of the toy situation, the words refused to follow her into the dream.

For her part, the girl had never known a world without words, could hardly fathom a difference between sounds and those things that exiled her from socializing, soccer games, and birthday parties. In spite of her close relationship with language, the girl had a taciturn disposition and was rather more interested in the flux of rearranging phrases that rippled along the curve of her wrist than in contemplating the suicidal lyrics of her classmates' bands. In this way she stumbled through adolescence, the teachers too intimidated by the annotations that crowded their smart boards to grade her with anything less than the highest of honors.

These teachers had some reason to feel daunted: By the time that she was twenty, the words had reconstructed poetry from almost all the romance languages, as well as from Greek, Russian, and Persian. Recently they had been migrating toward Chinese; over her left shoulder, one day, in the mirror, the girl had recognized the character for tree, squashed under a mole and between the Hebrew sign for life and the Omega. Although she had learned a little Spanish, she was always some considerable measure of behind with the words. They now scratched their mark into the most peculiar spaces, in the whites of her eyeballs through minute webbing of capillaries, or in the gums above her teeth, the constellations of freckles on her arms and back, spelling entire phrases. The Tao Te Ching climbed her spine from the bottom up; the poetry of Rumi tattooed on the underside of her tongue; the epic of Gilgamesh in its original Sumerian scrolled on the soles of her feet in a pale color just a half a tone lighter than her natural complexion.

A local journalist looking for a story once asked to interview her. He didn't say how he had found out about her, only offered a sweaty business card printed on an inkjet which left smears on his fingers when he gave it to her. Immediately, the phone number imprinted itself on the palm of her hand, and she, pointing at the life line upon which his name had scrolled, said, "Look. It's fate." The journalist had a tuft of brown hair that seemed to fall inevitably toward his left eye. He grabbed it with a gesture that made him look exasperated. He was a spindly thing, his pants tight at the waist but loose below the knee and around his hips, where she saw his bones protrude. He looked not quite mature enough to be alive, an adult in a child's body, pursuing ideas that seemed beyond his ability to conceive. As they talked, he watched the poetry of Sappho run its verse on her collarbone, its polyphonic orthography transmogrifying before him into the far less poetic, but infinitely simpler, Western alphabet. Before the day had run its course the two were sitting in her kitchen close enough to smell each other's coffee breath, and a cigarette burned in the ashtray untouched as his fingertips grazed her knuckles, and her chest bloomed Neruda verses.

He wrote an article, which he sold to *Time*, entitled "A Woman of Words," and it was all about her poetry and grace, as if she herself were the creations of genius that floated about the contour of her mouth when he thought only of poetry. But what mattered to her were the hours spent watching the names of all the constellations, from their ancient romantic origins to the unimaginative numerations of modern scientists, as they bloomed on her body with just his mention of the night. His attention was so new to her that she called it love. The names of stars glowed on the girl's abdomen as she climaxed, a bright halo of mantras lighting up like summer fireflies in the darkened bedroom. She held him in her arms, then, savoring the wordless eloquence of their breathing.

But like an original fairy tale, the romance came to a grim end. The journalist could not endure the constant assault of the loosened tufts of lost words on the unedited syntax of his articles, nor the annotations of the many things he did not know that spontaneously formed on the margins of the book he was writing as he read it out loud to her. One day, right after a TV interview in a morning show, she found him backstage, sucking on the thumb of a green room assistant who blinked her eyes at the invective which crackled and popped on her chin and forehead as the journalist muttered, "But you must have known; you must have felt us falling apart."

And although she stormed out with a tail of Shakespearean insults trailing after her "one may smile and smile and be a villain ..." like a comet, she burst and imploded on her own success. Her nervous breakdown occurred in Hollywood style, after her brief debut in a small supporting role with a famous Australian actress. Surrounded by so many thespians, the words burgeoned in unsightly bouquets on the girl's cheeks and eyelids, so that the makeup artists began to complain to the director about the difficulties of smoothing out her already dark and splotchy complexion, and eventually she was edited out of the film.

Scholars who had once exalted her in academic journals scoffed that she possessed no innate knowledge, publicly proclaiming her a paradigm of pop culture insipidness. A civil liberties group sued them for attempting to treat her body as a national archive (the lost Dead Sea Scroll appeared one day tattooed beneath her nipple), but the lawsuit was eventually dropped, and the public lost interest, and like so many starlets, she was a nobody again, left intoxicated and partly asleep in her rented London flat, at risk of choking on the vomit of her own verbiage.

One day, a single syllable cracked from a word and ended up dangling loosely from her ear, translucent, variegated by the light that struck it. It came alive when the wind blew in the appropriate tone. Then, the broken word set off all the rest of them, acting like a free radical, its unrestrained vibration dangerously catalyzing its sympathetic twins across the billions of syllables imprisoned in the neural net of manuscripts that had been weaving around and onto her body since birth, their chaotic symphony floating rapidly across invisible nets of reasoning, causing cataclysms of mistranslations down centuries of archiving and all the while humanity proceeding as if all were well....

She suspected nothing. Except one day, in a clothing store, the words radiating with chaotic insistence set off the alarm system. She held up her arms, one hand clutching the plastic bag that held a single garment (one plain colored T-shirt with no logo or print, the optimist in her offering the words a truce, a settlement), and the other clutching her receipt as evidence of her innocence, but they accused her of vandalism. She was frisked, thrown in jail, called a freak by the inmates, released. The end.

But not for the words: They set off lasers, beepers, cell phones, sent off entire novels in text messages to adolescents in Japan, wired speeches to charities in Peru and Michael Jackson jokes to eco-terrorists in Alaska. Once, when she had passed near a school, all one hundred and twenty Hindu words for god had imprinted themselves on the main wall in black carbon smears. The rising accusations of the scandalized teachers who ran to shield the children's eyes lodged like pinpricks into the back of her neck. As the words came and left her body, a dark cloud followed her so that more and more she resembled an adult-like, gender-corrected version of Pig-Pen.

The words had lost control of their own orbits, and they were no longer content or able to gyrate within the microcosm of the girl's body. She had grown to be a tall girl, almost five feet nine, yet the words, ever greedy for more surfaces to distend upon, crawled into her mouth at night and lowered themselves down her larynx until they reached her stomach. There they pushed nourishment aside, starving her until her skin stretched into long blankets of loose dermis, which the words immediately took care to paint in clever, interesting arrays of sentences that, in space-saving initiatives, held different meanings if read backward, forward, upside down, downside up, right to left, left to right, or diagonally.

And if someone spoke wisely out loud, the sentences, one by one, would burn a bright and vivid color on the loose skin around her hips, the equivalent of which did not exist in the spectrum of visible human colors, but which gave off a queer aura all the same. She knew that washing did not help, but all the same she scrubbed her skin and scrubbed and scrubbed, and out loud she pleaded with gods, medics, and doctors to find a cure for the unbearable curse, her body a human billboard incomprehensible to most. In the water, the words would tingle for a second or two and, like mosquito bites, itch just barely enough to be annoying, while the meaning and context would either float up with the faint scent of alcoholic ether or sink deeper into her dermis, where she suspected they mixed with her blood.

Each word carried its own gravity, but what weighed her down and made it difficult for her to sit up straight was when her parents, after endless counseling sessions, raccoon eyed and yellow toothed, told her in an exhausted pule of bad breath, "But, darling, you must be doing something to attract this; how will you ever find a partner with this condition of yours...."

What gave her the stoop in the shoulder, and later in life, a droop of her head that caused her long, long hair to drape around her face like curtains in a play, hiding away whatever final words of disparate wisdom ate away the paleness of her cheeks, were the contradictions of varied truths, the weight and flux of knowledge itself, and the curse of living within the orbit of ageless loquaciousness, surrounded by all that connected the human dimension with the divine, and her awareness of being just too small a vessel to contain it all, her share of understanding glaringly inadequate for the great task of damming the tidal flush of humanity's logorrhea.

And then one day, the words began to fight each other over their own meaning. Crowded curve to curl, period to comma, they bid for the remaining available real estate by surveying for redundancies, and they debated the discarding of various disputed translations of the Bible, dubious speeches attributed to Socrates, the entire United States tax code, chapters of the Pali Canons according to the Buddha. The words could not come to an accord about what had actually been written by Shakespeare and what might have been the work of his contemporaries, and scholarly debates on this subject were entirely too voluminous.

The girl was by then a middle-aged woman. She attempted to leave the country for an island in the Galapagos where she had heard no human (or language) lived. At the airport, however, she was careless, passing near a newsstand and allowing her eyes to roam over the colorful tile-displays of a magazine rack. It all happened quickly, shouts, bells ringing, a squad of undercover marshals surrounding her with their shouts of "Freeze!" slapping her chest like an open hand. She was taken to a tight metallic room with soundproof walls and asked questions about her luggage, her destination, her peculiar aura of syllables humming like hornets. As best as she could piece it out, the root word "bomb" had broken away from its "astic" attachment just as the final book of a bestselling vampire trilogy crowded in unexpectedly, causing a surge, and breaking several innocent free-standing dictionary entries (like bombastic), setting them ringing all at once.

"You said *bomb!*" insisted her bleach-haired interrogator. She tapped her pencil on a form, unimpressed by how the word imprinted itself in different languages on the girl's eyelids.

She didn't try to explain. Guantanamo seemed as good an idea as the Galapagos, where anyway she'd have had to cohabit with seals and compete for fish. She laid in her cell on the cot, relatively happy in spite of the sweltering heat of Cuba, the claustrophobic confinement, the mosquitoes and the vicious repetitions of the nursery rhymes that played at early morning hours through crackling loud speakers. At least now the immigration of words into the country of her body were limited to the questions of her interrogators, who were too unimaginative to come up with much that didn't already reside in her tear ducts. They asked her only things like, "Do you know this man?" holding up pictures of tawny, chicken-chinned radicals. They could have asked questions like, "Where does a mathematical equation exist?" and that would have been dangerous enough to her, but they seemed unaware of such possibilities.

She barely had enough strength to observe the escalating war between the words, collusions of crusaders against secular knowledge, the old science versus religion shibboleth, nursery rhymes sung to hide the horrors of pestilences, celebrity chef recipes challenged by Southern grandmothers. One after another, the words hurled themselves into prolonged hisses, dissonant vibrations reminiscent of Buddhist horns, rebel yells, yodels so dry that one morning she woke so dehydrated she was rushed to Medical and put on an IV, some words bouncing off of her toes in exodus, fed up, maybe, and looking for more fertile intellects than her own.

She longed for the wordless dreams she had as a child, to be able to hide somewhere where the creations of mind, the building blocks of matter, could not follow her or do much more than vanish like breath. Words: evanescent seeds of concrete nightmares like genocide, weaponry, torture, and reality shows. She would look down at the knot in her belly, the knot that once tied her to the breath of her mother, also the source of an illusion of knowledge relative only to human constructs. None of it was hers. But somehow all of it had passed through her, turning her into a living farrago, as if God had singled her out to stand as witness to the decadence of civilization.

She was found dead in her cell one morning, an unmistakable expression of relief etched in her rictus. It was said that her body, once a dance of skin-veils tattooed in cryptic verses that graced, in photographs, every pinot-noir-and-brie catered art-gallery reception around the globe, had turned, in the end, into an emaciated blur of red, incomplete fragments of sentences like unfinished thoughts tapering off at the edges of her long nails, a corporal testament of madness smelling faintly of sardines, a twig of human flesh destined to putrefaction, to bone dust and warble.

THE MADONNA OF THE DROWNED

Camilla leaned on the railing of the balcony, trying to keep her eyes on the rubber boat as it approached the coast. The gray thing appeared and disappeared through the mist and clouds or under a splashing wave. She and Enzo had spotted it earlier from their bedroom window, at first only a dot blinking in and out of the tall waves. The wind was strong this morning, the surf choppy. Camilla and Enzo had seen several of these rubber boats washed up on the beach, the Guardia Costiera patrolling the waters and fishing refugees out like so many ragged dolls. Just last month there was an incident off the coast, two hundred drowned because rough weather kept the Guardia Costera from getting to the refugees. It was all over the news. This morning, when they'd first sighted the rubber boat, Luca was awake. He'd seen it too. He came out of his room, yawning, and asked, "Are children on that boat? Are they going to be okay?"

Since the crisis started, Luca had seen things on TV, video clips of a wet camera in the rough sea, the Guardia Costera unable to get close enough for rescuing. Camilla had tried to keep him away, but Enzo, when he came home from work, stood in front of the TV, talking back to the newscasters: "They are all such incompetents." And when the politicians discussed the difficulty of caring for them, "This is the legacy of Berlusconi's government. Send them back? Like we had nothing to do with the mess that got them to this." If his brother, Tommaso, came up to the flat to play cards or talk over a grappa, the two of them would join in on the debate against the television: "Slippery and slow," Enzo declared, his arms crossed over his chest. "Criminals in the parliament," Tommaso chimed in. She couldn't say how much Luca understood, but surely he had heard them, maybe even seen some of the footage.

This thing between the television and the men was like a song, the ones behind the screen singing a rift, and the men chiming in like a choir. Nothing changed. Nothing was ever accomplished. On Sundays, Camilla dropped a ten-euro bill in the church's collection box, another note for the endless song. Ten euros could help no one. For her, there was no consolation in blaming the EU for not opening up their borders. The ten euros never even made her feel better about herself.

Enzo's and Camilla's apartment was on the top floor of a three-story building, on a hill. It was a windy day, and the boat was clearly in trouble. They saw a second boat coming behind the first, two gray stains, tipping with the waves like dying beasts with hundreds of brown claws clinging to the deflating edges. Camilla tugged Luca to her bosom and pushed a kiss between his bangs. He was still soft from sleeping and yawning large.

"Go to my bedroom," she told him. "In the left drawer under the beds there are blankets. Bring them to me."

Downstairs, in front of the portal, Signora Giovanna, the baker, waved. "Signora," the baker said. "More are coming, even today, you see?"

"I see everything from up here."

Their little town, once tranquil and remote, was pregnant with tented camps and washed-up corpses. Up here, she had the best theater seats to the drama. Only, she didn't like the show. She missed the silence of winters when there were no tourists around. She didn't like this symphony of puttering vans and mopeds, whirring helicopters, honking Guardia Costera ships and tugboats.

Giovanna clapped her hands together. "Why does God send us this misery? What do we have here? Nothing. They come like locusts. God save us." She crossed herself.

"We are bringing blankets and old clothes to the beach," she told Giovanna. "Luca is getting them now. If you have anything you want to donate…"

"If I give away any more, I am going to have to ask for government assistance myself."

Camilla had been like Giovanna. She had prayed about the crisis to the Madonna di Porto Salvo, the Madonna protector of Lampedusa. There was a statue of her under the water, offshore. This Madonna was supposed to console the drowned and the lost, to usher them to heaven, but – she was ashamed of this now – Lampedusa was not heaven. She prayed that the refugees would go elsewhere. She prayed that her village return to what it was like before the boats began to wash up. She wanted to cross the street and stare into a man's eye and know him and his family. She wanted the park to be empty, the train stations spotted only with the occasional, local, beggar.

One day, the body of a toddler washed up on the shore. The photograph was on every newspaper and magazine. The toddler was dressed like Luca would have been at his age, like one of her own children: black polished shoes, an argyle sweater vest, socks pulled up to the knees. A little man dressed for school, lying on the sand face down. The image of that boy haunted her in sleep. She began to go through the old blankets and baby clothes she'd saved for when her oldest son, Mario, would have children. Still, each time she parted from something she felt a pinch in her abdomen, in a tender spot of uncertainty and frailty.

She held the image of that drowned boy in her head as she approached the beach with Luca, making her way down the stone path, through the hillside creepers, the sea getting louder, the green foam seething as the waves crashed.

Suffering was a repulsive ghost, not like what they showed on television through the skillful frame of the cameramen, a suffering sanitized for public viewing, a beautiful agony, pale and tranquil like a work of art. The suffering she saw stank of rotting meat. It was ugly bones and sores, bad breath and maggots. And hunger, a violent sort of hunger that ate at its victims from within.

The rubber boat was in tatters and flailing bodies and clothes washed up on the rocks, raked by the sea, tall hissing sprays of foam rising from the crags as the waves broke against the back of the island. On a sunny day, the *caletta* could be a paradise of waters so transparent that the fishermen's boats and yachts crowding into the lagoon looked like they were suspended on air. But today the sky was gray, the sea livid like a bruise, and angry. The sea today spat people out of its belching wet mouth.

Camilla saw the pregnant girl, as if her eyes had known to pluck her out from the splashing limbs, waterlogged clothes bloating around the wading desperate who had fallen from the boat. Some of the rescue helpers, too, had jumped in the water, and they struggled against the currents and with their own waterlogged clothes as they swam toward the fallen ones.

The pregnant girl had reached shallower waters, a hand holding her curved belly, stumbling and trembling as she waded on toward shore, her hands bleeding as she held herself up against the crags, the waves making her progress slow and dangerous. Immediately, Camilla knew that it was the girl's time, that her waters had broken already, maybe on that boat. The pregnant girl was shining obsidian in the twilight, bent a little, a wet dark stalk overwhelmed by the mistral wind inside the great cosmos that was the womb. Camilla felt the stranglehold of the girl's cramps in her own belly as she watched the girl splashing toward shore. She was a dark Madonna, a Venus arising from the sea, foam at her thighs, at the beaded bracelets around her thin wrist, around her long, stork-like neck, but when she raised her face to the rescuers who bustled on the shore with blankets, water, and medical kits, she fell to her knees with a cry.

Camilla grasped Luca's hand, feeling for the boy's cold wet fingers. "Look, that girl is about to deliver."

Luca hadn't yet set eyes on the girl, on her bloodstained clothes. She had strangely piercing tigress eyes, a color like dying suns. The girl dragged herself toward shore, mouthing whispers of agony in a language Camilla failed to grasp. Not French, certainly not Italian. Camilla felt the words in her heart, mother-to mother, connecting not from intellect or understanding, but from the depths of her womb.

Luca brought her back to the moment, wincing, "*Aiiiah*, Mamma." He jerked his hand from her tight grip. She'd been inadvertently squeezing him. She looked to her left, to her right, the beach busy already with people running to and from the water, loud horns announcing the Guardia Costiera, hovering helicopters batting their helixes overhead and raising long veils of sand. "Help," she cried. "Help that girl, help her."

Camilla was a small woman. She waded in the water toward the girl, crying, "Help, help, please," but no one heard her, no one but the young goddess in the water, shiny like a stone, angular and hard and surprisingly light.

"Help her," Camilla shouted, as she grabbed the girl's arms and lifted her. Out into the deep sea the helicopters hovered around those who were still at sea, the gleaming backs of the capsized boats rising against the ship's aft. "Help us." Her voice was lost, though, over the din. So many of the refugees needed help. So many came ashore, young men whose skulls looked washed out of all life by the sea, eyes still wide with terror.

Move, Camilla told herself, fighting the thunderstorm inside her own head. *Do something*. The pregnant girl felt fragile in her arms, a precious work of bones and skin that might break with another tug. The belly's contractions made the girl cry out with an almost inhuman voice, but Camilla could see that the baby would be born, that it would not be put off another minute.

The girl had fallen to her knees. No longer looking at Camilla, she hung her head between her shoulders and wailed like it was up to the strength of her voice to save her baby from drowning. Blood gushed from her and all around her men and women splashed by, blood staining the sea foam and sand.

Camilla eased the girl to sit, and then to lie back. Luca, helpless, stood calf-deep in water.

"Luca, set those blankets down and go fetch one of those men in the white wind jackets."

The girl screamed again, between her legs a thick stream of blood.

"Mamma," Luca cried as he pointed at the blood.

"Go get your Papa, or one of the people with the Red Cross sign, go."

Luca ran, likely relieved to be given something to do – or at least, glad to be given a reason to run. Camilla felt better seeing him go, his legs kicking up sand.

A volunteer worker in a white wind jacket was helping to carry an old woman to shore, her mouth open and gaping as if she were lacking air. Camilla grabbed the volunteer by his elbow.

"I need help or both this woman and the baby are going to die."

"We are working as fast as we can, signora," he said, but he looked at the girl, and shouted a name. Near the shore, another volunteer looked up and saw.

"Hurry," Camilla said. The girl in her arms cried out loud, and for a moment, it seemed, her agony swept above all other agonies, and the Universe quieted to hear her: *Hush now, a child is coming, a life.* Camilla crawled to sit behind the woman, arranging the girl's head to rest between her breasts. The smell of her unwashed skin mingled with the pungent one of blood, with the saltiness of the water. Camilla gently arranged the girl's matted strands of hair, soggy and wooly. She whispered like a mother, "It's all right. It's okay. The baby is coming. Be brave."

It took hours for the baby to be born, agonizing hours during which Camilla endured the weight of the girl on her lap, coaching her, coaxing the baby out of her with gentle words. The two volunteers, the doctor, the Guardia Costiera, had wanted her to go away, but the girl clung to her elbow with her feeble fingers, her will to live stronger than her body, and Camilla stayed, brushing the girl's matted hair from her forehead, from her mouth.

Hours, painful hours later, the child came out, squirming and screaming with a force that astounded the emaciated blanket-clad refugees shivering on the beach, some of them even too weak to hold a cup of broth to their lips, but not too weak to smile, or to nod, eyes wide and bloodshot with too much sun and salt. Life had prevailed, even through this. Life had reaffirmed them, so they nodded, acknowledging the gift of one of their own, spared from the sea.

The volunteers held up the baby and laughed. "It's a girl. Look. It's a girl." The mother managed a faint smile, held her, and settled her on her chest before she blacked out into sleep, the two volunteers fussing around her. "She has to be moved." "But there is no room in the hospital." "Well, she can't stay here." "Where is she supposed to go?" "The train station. They are moving people to the train station."

"The train station? But it's barbarous. What are you thinking?"

"They have cots there, *signora*, facilities. In a few days maybe we can move her to a hotel."

The volunteer explained what Camilla already knew, what the TV said, what the newspapers said. There was no room back at the camp, and here, they could not stay.

When the rafts had first begun to wash up in Lampedusa, the Red Cross, failing to anticipate how serious and how quickly the crisis would devolve, had set the first of the refugees up in the thousand-year-old rock dwellings, the so-called *dammusi*. They were reinforced below ground with steel bunkers built during World War II. Once, when Camilla was younger she'd had to hide in those *dammusi*. Libya had shot a scud missile at the American military base, and the Americans had fled the island as a result, leaving the mayor of Lampedusa certain that Libya was going to invade. The church bells had never clanged so loud, and everyone in town was led down the cave dwellings into the bunkers.

The darkness was oppressive, the air rarefied. And though she was no child then, she remembered holding tight to *Nonna* Maria, finding comfort in her *nonna*'s familiar smell of orange rinds and vanilla, and in that voice that whispered, "*Calma, non c'e' niente, non e' nulla, vedrai.*" She couldn't imagine a girl who'd just given birth crowded into one of those dark caves.

Some refugees, because they didn't have papers, went to camp in the woods, near the beach coves, their colorful blankets spread out under the umbrella pines. Camilla used to drop used clothes and toys there, until she began to notice how the camps were patrolled by young men, looking too healthy to be refugees, too well fed, their quick glances slowing only for the backside of girls, sometimes for boys, too. They were looking for commodities, for slaves. Displaced by the war, impossible to trace, these bodies were already dead as far as governments were concerned, and therefore, disposable.

"She will have to get on a list."

Camilla took a look at the sleeping girl. All she had was what she wore, a tattered dress, wet and half-torn, soiled with feces because packed so tight on those boats they couldn't move without tipping it over. Of course, she didn't have papers. She'd be put on a boat or an airplane and taken to who-knew-where.

The girl slept in Camilla's arms. Camilla let her rest, the newborn baby nestled between them, crying small, bothered cries, but soothed somewhat by her mother's naked breasts, by the roaring ocean and the white noise of talk and movement all around.

Later she would say to Enzo that she'd had no choice. Enzo too, had no choice, finding her on the beach, the tide low, the girl still sleeping, nestled in Camilla's lap, an ebony gift from the sea. And the baby, a blessing, surely, at Camilla's and Enzo's age? Luca was getting ready for middle school, but a baby, a new baby, was a blessing straight from the Madonna of Porto Salvo.

"We have had plenty of blessings, already," Enzo grumbled. "And where should we put her, in the laundry room?" But he, too, held up the tiny baby, so small that her head rested completely in the palm of his large hand, and she glimpsed the smile tugging at his lips under his mustache, the baby such a fragile thing in his hands, so precious, so needy of comforting and shelter.

"Luca won't mind sharing, won't you, Luca?" Luca nodded solemnly. He'd been excited to show the girl his space, his bunk bed with the Pixar covers, the wall decal with Harry Potter characters, and his most prized possession, his starship *Enterprise* drone, a gift from his big brother Mario that he got for his ninth birthday.

The girl's name was Nesreen. She was Eritrean. Camilla thought she may have said that she was seventeen years old but wasn't sure. She had asked the girl to make the figure with her fingers, but the girl looked uncertain, embarrassed even, after the first attempt pulling the baby up from the bed and nuzzling her. When they had asked her to bathe, Camilla had to show her how to wait for the boiler to warm up. The girl had gasped when the water had gotten hot, speaking fast in her native tongue, her incomprehensible, tangled tongue. Camilla poured the rose-scented bubble bath into five inches of water, encouraging Nesreen with her hands, with smiles. Nesreen dabbed bubbles on her chin and over her eyebrows. It was the first and only time Camilla saw her smile.

Nesreen's breasts were swollen with milk, and her hips were generous enough, in spite of her gauntness, and her face folded near the nose and around the eyes, an effect of hunger, the volunteers had told her, but Nesreen was a child, in the way she moved, in the way her old-sun eyes devoured the baby, her nervous hands both expert and clumsy as she tried to swaddle her in the T-shirts Camilla had rustled up from Enzo's drawer. Luca's old baby clothes had already gone to the donation bin, years ago. Camilla saw the marks of abuse on the girl: a ridged scar in her inner thigh, bruises over her arms and chest. Later she pointed at the scar. "That? What is that?"

Nesreen made a gesture, with her face, with her eyes, with the way her chin moved just. It was as if she'd spoken, said something eloquent and thorough. Camilla was not to ever ask again. She was never going to learn the whole story. Camilla had read the papers, anyway.

***

Nesreen named the baby Aya. It sounded like an exclamation of pain, like Luca when he scraped his knees playing soccer or burned himself trying to use the grill. Surely there had been enough pain in Nesreen's life? Wouldn't naming the baby after pain bring more trouble?

Aya was a small, purple baby, and she cried and cried all night long, a colicky baby. Nesreen stayed awake, bouncing the baby, but Camilla, too, stayed awake, and Enzo, and Luca. The next day, Enzo, who worked on the fishermen's peer, was tired all day. He came home grumpy complaining that the pasta was overcooked, the tomato sauce too salty. He got up without finishing his plate and turned on the television, and the baby cried, and Enzo drummed his fingers on the couch, until he got up and said he was going to see Tommaso. Camilla showed Nesreen how to bicycle the baby's legs, how to massage her little tummy to soothe the pain.

Every day Camilla walked downhill to the town's center, to the mayor's office, to ask about opportunities for Nesreen. Always the same noncommittal answer, citing of issues beyond local laws, the French, the Germans, the Americans alternatively, like stubborn gods, answering with silence the bureaucrats' invocations and curses. At the volunteer camp, it was the same, Nesreen's name on a list with a thousand others might as well have been an ink blot. Who knew if it was her real name?

The line was always long, and usually Camilla didn't pay attention to the masses of young men and women seeking help, or to the exasperated, irritable volunteers that corralled them or referred them elsewhere. Then, Camilla began to notice a quiet man, one of the refugees. At least so she thought by the color of his skin. He stood near the entrance, an unlit cigarette dangling from his lips. Sometimes he stood there alone, sometimes with others. She couldn't say how old he was. Maybe thirty-five, maybe eighteen, the way their eyes looked so old and mean in some of them. This one looked neat and shaven, not desperate and ruffled like the others. She began to notice that she could spot him in a crowd, and he seemed to know right away she was looking at him. He'd look up, unflinching, stare right back at her. If he was with company, he'd say something to the other boys or men. And they'd nod and shout things she did not understand except by the tone. What? Women without veils? Women looking at men in the eye? She touched her head, her uncovered graying head. The man grinned, his fingers touching the cigarette near his lips. He nodded like they'd just transacted business.

***

Nesreen's breast was dry after only the first week. The baby was inconsolable and hot with fever. The baby's crying had stolen so many hours of their sleep that Enzo had shouted at his contract crewman at work. The crewman had complained to administration and Enzo was sent home, while Luca, too, had fallen asleep in class and the teacher had called home concerned. "To take a stranger like that into your home," the teacher had the audacity to tell Camilla.

"Was Luca ever asked what he thought about it?"

"Luca? He's a child. What does he understand. Besides, he's very generous," Camilla said, her voice high-pitched. "He is a Christian child with Christian values. You could learn something from him." She hung up.

The next week, the principal called. No mention was made of Nesreen, but questions came about how much attention Enzo and Camilla were paying to Luca: had they noticed that Luca had suffered drops in his grades? Did they know he fell asleep in class and sometimes lashed out at his teachers? Why weren't they paying attention? Clearly something had happened in the boy's life to cause such a change in his attitude. He wasn't the same.

Nesreen learned four words of Italian: *Latte, bambina, ciao, cioccolata.* The two women had invented a language of gestures and sounds, grimaces, scowls, smiles, and winks that barely got them through basic communication: Are you hungry? Is the baby all right? This is how you...

"Crazy women." Enzo scowled with his arms crossed, watching Camilla show Nesreen how to work the washer, how to turn on the boiler for hot water, and where to hang the clothes to dry where the birds wouldn't get to them. Then, Camilla went to the grocery store.

When she came back, Nesreen was outside, near the corner, almost unseen behind a large rosemary bush. Nesreen's head was bent as she listened to a man who was talking to her in a low but persistent tone. Nesreen's knees were bent, too. She was not quite squatting, not quite standing, leaning against the wall like the house depended on her holding it up. Camilla watched them, grocery bags in hand. She recognized the man. She'd seen him before, in the woods where she delivered the clothes, or at the camp, yes, at the camp. He sensed her now. He turned, the white of his eyes brilliant against the black of his irises, a contrast to the dark smoothness of his face. He had such eyes! Such hard eyes! Nesreen, seeing her, wiped her face, her nose. "Signora."

"Go inside," Camilla said, nudging her chin to the door. Nesreen hurried inside.

The man's mouth tugged at a corner. He came to her, a hand in the pocket of his jeans, new, clean jeans. His shirt, too, looked freshly pressed.

"What do you want with the girl?" she demanded.

The man's eyes brightened. Camilla saw something move behind them, a thought that might have frightened her if she knew what it was.

"What do you want with the girl?" he threw back at her.

"She's not yours," she said.

"She's not yours," he echoed back. He grinned, big teeth, yellow and shining. He was enjoying this child's game.

There was a silent impasse. Finally, he said, "You a hero?" That cigarette again. He'd pulled it out of his jeans, held it to his lips and grinned. "You must be very brave, *signora*." He was standing very close to her now, his eyes slits as he stared right at her, making her look down, in spite of herself. "A very brave, compassionate mother."

"You be careful," she said.

"Yes, you be careful." He nodded and turned his back, crossing the street with a bounce, a kind of strut.

She went upstairs, shaking a little, thinking about whether or not to tell Enzo. She found Nesreen in the laundry room. She was on her knees, in her lap a faint orange pile of rags. Her face was wet with tears. *"Ch'e' successo?*" She knelt beside her: Are you sick? Is the baby sick? Did he want something, that man? The girl held out a pair of shorts, the uneven green color dull but spoiled all the same into a putrid yellow green, like a sick baby's poop. Camilla recognized Luca's soccer shorts, deformed by the too hot temperature, by the wrong combination of detergent and bleach. Through the pile of ruined clothes, she picked out two of Enzo's work shirts, Luca's good gabardine pants, and her own silk dress, one that used to belong to her mother.

"They're only stuff," she said to the girl patting her shoulder, trying to think of the excuses she'd have to make up for Enzo, for the shirts.

The weeks passed on like this: Luca went into his room, straight from school, locking himself in. The baby cried at night, waking up everyone. Camilla got up because Enzo huffed, because he shouted into his pillow, because Luca called from his bed, "Mamma? Mamma?" with nightmares, he said, about the baby taking his mother from him.

"Aya is just a little girl, a gift from God. She can't take anything from you."

"I don't like her," Luca said. "I don't like Nesreen either. Make them go away."

Nesreen tried to learn to talk; she tried to learn to clean things, to use the appliances. She burned milk on the stove; she dropped a whole bag of rice, kernels turning up everywhere for days, under the chairs, in the baby's clothes, under the couch pillows; she tried to iron Aya's bibs and burned one. She said, "*Signora.*" She said, "*Scusi tanto.*" She said, "*Non capisco, veramente,*" and money went missing from Camilla's purse and from Enzo's wallet, and bruises appeared on Nesreen on her side where they would not be seen except when Nesreen did her morning prayers to Mecca, the hand-me-down shirts she wore hitching up her back as she touched her head down to the mat.

Camilla thought about calling the police. She thought about how the police would react to Nesreen, without papers, in her house, about what Nesreen would say to officers who might take away her child. At whom would she point the finger to explain her bruises?

Over time, Camilla spoke less and less, she said, "Not like this, Nesreen," and "Let it be. I'll take care of it," and then nothing, because every word was a fishbone in her throat, every thought a bitter fish-scale taste, and Nesreen's eyes like old suns seemed like two curses stuck in the head of a girl who Camilla suspected would never outlive her own youth.

***

Giovanna, the baker, slipped an extra bread loaf in her bag. "Do you know what I saw on TV? They complain. They don't like it here. They want to go north, to France, to Germany. Because we give them no jobs; you see the irony? They live in luxury hotels, some of them even have swimming pools, but they say they want more. They want opportunities, education. Here, they just wait." Giovanna made a dismissive gesture with her hand, her mouth set in a solemn frown. "Maybe they're right; who knows? There are no jobs here, that's for sure, not even for us. So, some of them tip the ferryman, the fisherman, the man with a boat." Giovanna rubbed the tips of her fingers together to mean a money exchange, looking meaningfully at Camilla.

"And what do you suggest I do? Abandon a girl with a new baby? Like a dog, kick it to the curb when you're tired of playing with it; is that right?"

Giovanna raised both her hands. "Oh, no, I'm not saying anything about you. You're a saint, everyone knows that. Camilla the good Samaritan of Lampedusa. You took in a stranger, a girl and a baby, in your home, a young girl with two men in your house, you can't possibly want advice from me."

"Two men? Luca is a child. What are you saying, Giovanna, eh?"

It was cruel, to put such thoughts into her head. Camilla didn't know how to explode with all that she had inside her. "And what have you done," she shouted. "Eh? What have you done to help?"

"I mind my own business," Giovanna said.

"It's everyone's business," Camilla shouted. By then a crowd had gathered, women talking all at once, offering advice. "*Ma no, signora!* Giovanna is only saying... Who knows, after all... We don't know who these people are...."

Camilla had wanted to make a grand gesture about it, tipping the decorative bread basket, but when the old bread clattered to the ground, shattering, the silence after all that bickering fell heavy, like God's judgment. Then, Giovanna with her hands together in prayer: "*Ma chi te lo fa fa?*" Who is making you do it?

***

The thought came to her in sleep, waking her, her eyes trained on the ceiling as if waiting for God's finger to point at her, to expose what she already knew: that Giovanna was right, she was no saint; she could not open her heart as wide as she thought she could, not even for a child. And all the guilt in the world was not going to change what had to happen.

Hours before morning, she led Nesreen by the hand, the baby swaddled up in one of Luca's T-shirts, and the pizzi, the precious crochet works that Nonna Maria had crafted so carefully with her fingers, were wrapped in paper and tucked under her arm, a small gift of wealth for her daughters and granddaughters, now a gift for Nasreen. The girl, if she wasn't a complete fool, would know to sell the work for good money, if she had understood beyond her *"Mi scusi tanto, signora."* Nesreen said nothing all through their short journey to the marina, and the baby, Aya's big eyes stared at the moon, so serious, as if she'd acquired already the wisdom that so eluded her mother.

Enzo's Christmas bonus went to the captain. The cash was for Nesreen, and for the baby, formula and a pack of diapers.

They shared a blessing between them: *"Che Dio ti protegga."*

The boat moved silently toward the fishing barge. The only sound besides the splashing oars was the baby's halting cry, like a night bird. Underneath a sliver of moon, beneath the dark waters, the Madonna's arms of stone extended upward to welcome them, the wretched and the abandoned.

WHAT THEY KNOW

Checking her face in the mirror, she feels him move behind her, his attention absorbing the space between them. "What?" she says. He doesn't answer, turns to the mirror and yawns, right earbud in his ear, left one dangling at his shoulder.

Later, at the gas station, a woman's glance slides up her calves to the back of her skirt. She wants to say something, but the woman turns away, enters the shop and talks to a man whose chin drops low, moving close to her face. They both turn to the parking lot, to her at the gas pump, where she presses rhythmically on the handle for a few last drops. The man whispers something…They both laugh.

In class, it happens again. She lectures. A student in the back laughs. He thinks she can't see him, the way that something funny hits him in the chest with a jolt. With his elbow, he nudges someone who is cradling a phone under the desk. The boy talks to the other softly, lips stretched wide, teeth showing. She can hear the boy's voice but not what he says.

What? What is it? Is her nose bleeding? Did she spit? Is it her accent?

Out loud: Something funny you want to share? There is a steel-edge to the question, even through her smile, her voice like a gloved hand seizing a throat.

The class becomes quiet and alert, cats smelling a kill. The boy: a casual shake of the head, a nah' slipping out like a sigh. But it happens again, later. The one with the cell phone looks up suddenly, face slack, as if he's just coming out of sleep. His mouth forms an "oh" he breathes out, not quite like a laugh, like the beginning of a laugh. The boys turn to each other, share a grin: it slides from one's mouth to the other's, telegraphed, wired.

She's a surface of splinters and edges. She's shards of glass glued on cardboard with spit.

In the bathroom, she checks her makeup, her clothes. Looks up her nose.

Checks her teeth. Maybe her breath?

In the parking lot, a colleague waves, says, "You okay?"

"Why?"

"Just asking."

At dinner, her husband keeps his eyes on his plate, then notices her and folds his hands under his chin. He asks if she's all right, if something's happened.

"Students stare at me. People look at me like there something wrong with me."

His hand reaches out to hers, pats her knuckles once, twice. "No one's looking at you," he says.

That night, in a dream, she walks through the narrow halls of a funhouse, her feet sinking into foam. Her body stretches in the warped space of mirrors, her belly blowing out, a helium pregnancy. Her neck is a string of molten silver that stretches thin as she moves and snaps into two teardrops that kiss and shrink away.

ICE STORM

For weeks, Duke had tried to get Ellie excited about their trip to Tybee Island. He'd hoped that getting out of New York would give them a break from the sub-zero temperatures they could expect in February. Savannah was in the 70's when he'd checked the weather website and made the reservation, but a cold front had come through, and now the radar forecasted clear skies, but temperatures in the low 40's. Ellie had tried to talk him into canceling the trip with that curmudgeon-like tone she had used on him in the last fifteen years of their marriage, but Duke refused to be let down. Besides, their deposit was nonrefundable. Coming out of the shower with wet hair, raising his arms in victory, he'd boomed, "Winter is coming."

Ellie had looked up from her laptop with a tentative smile, gazing at Duke above her purple glasses, which had slid to the end of her nose. Duke had tried to plant a kiss on her neck, but Ellie kept right on typing.

"You're dripping," she'd said, moving her laptop closer.

"Winter is coming," Duke repeated the joke, pumping his fist, and was rewarded for his effort with a sidelong glance from Ellie, eyes fixed on his beer belly. When they had first met, almost thirty years ago, he boasted those so-called washboard abs that girls seemed to like, spending every spare moment at the gym and wasting no occasion to show them off in the presence of women he liked, but, he thought, looking down at the hairy swell that his stomach had become, he hadn't let himself go as much as Ellie had. She seemed to read his mind, running her fingers through her hair, where an inch of silver-gray evidenced the months since her last coloring appointment. She got up, shutting her laptop with a snapping sound that matched the way she looked at him. His eyes followed Ellie into the bedroom until she shut the door behind her.

Duke had been dry for eight years, but since the men from the government delivered the letter that had destroyed Ellie, he had begun to collect miniature liquor shots from the gas station on his way back from work. When he heard the soft clicking of Ellie's fingers on her laptop, he went to the bathroom and from the toilet tank, he selected one from a collection of Bourbon, Gin, and Vodka, which he pulled dry with one gulp and then discarded in the garbage without Ellie ever stopping her clicking or her shouting into her cellphone.

When the car finally pulled up to the cottage in Tybee, Duke had been without drink for hours. The rental agent stood on the doorsteps to greet them, "Hey, y'all. Welcome to Tybee." Behind her, the cottage, painted in pastels and sunlight, cheered them with its shrimp décor. Island kitsch hung from the door.

They both smiled at the rental agent, but Ellie was on her cellphone as soon as she stepped in, dropping her bag in the living room on the denim couch, letting Duke nod to Arlene as she gave him the rundown on the island, the distance to the beach (four blocks through the park), the nearest grocery store (off Jones at the streetlight) and some nice restaurants in the area. All through it, Duke smiled his Viagra ad smile, looking at the arrow hanging near the door that had the word beach carved in it.

"Well, dang," he said as he inspected the property. "Isn't this cute, Ellie?"

Ellie yelled into her phone: "Tell them to hold off on sending the galley. Tell them to wait until I get back."

Duke shrugged. "Work," he told Arlene.

"This cottage here's one of my favorites," said Arlene. "Y'all got the right idea coming down in winter. Let's hope that ice storm doesn't spoil everything. The news said we might get some weather down here."

Arlene was a tallish woman, thick-boned, large-breasted, and pretty like the women in Duke's family. The moment Duke detected the twang in her voice he slipped inside his native North Carolina talk. The tightness around his neck that had followed him from their cramped waiting at the gates, delayed in New York by snow, and then again in Atlanta by ice, began to melt and warm with the first words Arlene had spoken.

"Kind of cold for these parts, ain't it?" he observed.

"Oh, it'll warm up," said Arlene. "You give it a couple of days."

Ellie, who had sat on the queen-size bed in the living room, opened her laptop and began to type.

"It'll warm up," Arlene said, louder, looking through the door at Ellie. "This ice storm's just a fluke." She slapped Duke twice on his arm. "We'll find ways for y'all to get warm, don't worry," she said and broke into a big, open-mouthed laugh that put Duke in mind of a rum toddy.

"You got any booze stacked into one of those cabinets, Arlene?" he said in a voice that matched hers in bigness. "Listen to that, Ellie," he called out. "Arlene's got the cure for the cold."

"This is not what it's usually like," Arlene said. "It's that arctic spell from the north. Did you bring us the cold, Duke? Did you do that?" Arlene leaned toward him, her warm hand on his arm.

He laughed and wanted a drink very badly. He could feel his eyes getting into a squint.

"Did you hear that Ellie? Arlene's blaming us for the cold."

Ellie was typing away on her computer. "Internet's slow," she said.

When Arlene left a little later, Duke inspected the kitchen, half hoping that the previous residents might have forgotten a bottle. He opened the cabinets under the sink.

Ellie didn't stop typing. She called out, "Duke? What are you doing?"

"Look at this place, Ellie," said Duke, hearing himself slide into the Southern drawl that had softened his speech in the earlier years of his life.

The bathroom cabinets had no booze either. Everything was clean and well organized. There was a bucket on a stool near the sink with neatly folded towels. The sink itself was painted with fishes. Duke looked at the fish in the sink and listened to Ellie's typing. He closed his eyes, and the clicking of her fingers on the keys were like a bees' buzz, or worse, like the hum of an air conditioner or artificial lights, the sound of loneliness. He left the bathroom and went out to the living room, where he looked into every cabinet to find only well-stacked dishes and clean cups.

The second bedroom with two twin beds had large pink plastic shrimps hanging from a coat hanger. A straw chair painted moss green leaned against the window, where sunshine streamed in and filled the room in spite of the cool.

Duke stood before the twin beds, his fists popped on his hips. Two bright orange blankets had been folded at the base of each of the twin beds. The quilts that covered them bloomed with swirls of red, yellow, and blue polka dots. Duke stood beside the coat hanger with the shrimp and stared at the bed and at the sunlight that streamed through the window. He had stopped drinking eight years ago after a stroke. The last sip of vodka he'd had today was hours ago, when the flight delay had stranded them another two hours at JFK, and he'd managed to sneak a shot at the bar while Ellie went to the ladies' room.

That was why he could not understand.

He was sober when he saw the two pre-adolescent girls wearing socks jumping on the mattresses, one atop each of the twin beds, their ponytails swinging up behind them and dropping down after them. Their giggles filled the room, the mattresses squeaked and the headboards banged weakly against the wall.

Duke wasn't dreaming this. He wasn't even hallucinating it. His mind had conjured the image out of a wish, or a memory, and projected it through his eyes into this room. The girls wore shorts and tight T-shirts, one with a snapping turtle, the other a simple white T-shirt with no logo.

"Hey, Ellie, take a look at this place," he called out, watching the girls jump. Ellie padded up behind him.

"Fascinating," Ellie said, laptop in hand. "Internet's weak."

Ellie's presence had made the girls seem fainter now, only the sound of the mattress squeaking under their weight echoing in Duke's mind. Duke watched the girls jump quietly, their smiles beckoning him to step away from the cool February day, from the unheated cottage, from Ellie, into their promise of summer and sand.

There was a guestbook on the credenza near the twin bedroom. In the guestbook, Duke found the scribble of a child under the date *August 8, 2013*. The pen had made a hard trench onto the lined paper, and someone had drawn in arrows to point to fainter initials under the same page, saying *Nana* and *Mama*.

August of last year had been when Ellie and Duke received the letter. Men in uniform had delivered it, with Jessie's name typed in with the rest of the news, and the condolences, and the praise for the sacrifice that Jessie had made for her country.

Duke closed the guestbook. He walked out of the cottage and into the chill street without a word to Ellie. It was cold for February for Georgia, but the cold made it real for Duke to be walking these oak-draped streets, to smell the sea even four blocks away, to pass cottage after cottage with boats in the yard and trees decorated with shrimp and fish signs, to the convenience store on the corner, where he picked up shampoo, ketchup, mayonnaise, and a tube of toothpaste before he hovered over the cooler. He chose a couple of six-packs, and at the last minute, he picked up two frozen bean burritos. At the cash register, he watched a round-faced, dimpled girl ring up his toothpaste and mayonnaise.

"Say," he said to the girl at the cash register. "Are there ghosts on the island? I know Savannah's famous for it, but here?" He waited for the girl to look up, which she did slowly, processing the question.

"I think so." Her ponytail bobbed as she nodded. She slid the mayonnaise into a plastic bag. "There's some ghost tours on the island you could check out."

"We're from New York," Duke explained, leaning with his elbow on the counter. "My wife's a ghost junkie." He felt the need to amend. "She watches *Ghost Hunters*, all the shows."

In fact, Ellie never watched TV. Duke tried to conjure in his mind a recent memory of Ellie doing anything other than shouting into a cell phone or typing into her laptop, but the only memory that came was the one on the day of the letter.

The girl hummed low. "Oh, she'll love Savannah. Savannah's one of the most haunted towns in America." She crossed her arms over the counter, and Duke knew they were going to be chatting a while.

By the time he got home, it was dark, and Ellie was sprawled on the couch, wrapped in a green blanket and watching television. Duke had drunk the six-pack sitting outside the convenience store, sucking down each can and slam-dunking it into the garbage can. From time to time, the cashier girl, Billy, came out to smoke a cigarette, bouncing on her toes and wrapping her sweater closer to her body.

"Cold." She looked out into the livid cumulus and sucked her cigarette. "It ain't like this, usually. Swear it's the perfect day for ghosts."

She had a small chin but a heart-shaped face that Duke thought some men might think beautiful.

Duke downed another beer. In this way, he finished the first six-pack, and put away half of a second one.

By the time he stumbled back inside the cottage, he was more than a little drunk.

"Hey, Ellie." He waved big when he walked in, as if she couldn't see him.

"Heat's not working," she said.

"You're not working." He dropped what was left of the six-pack, along with the mayonnaise and the ketchup and the toothpaste and the bean burritos on the floor next to the couch and straddled Ellie.

Ellie tried to poke her head to see through his arms at the Olympics. "This girl," she said, looking at the television. "Look at her. She's so young. Reminds me of our girls. How do they make them do that?"

Duke turned to the television just in time to see the Russian skater perform her final spin. The girl had small eyes, short neck, and a muscular body. She kicked her leg up above her head and held onto her ankle and spun, her leg slightly arched inward, looking like something mechanical, impossible, a music box wound too tight.

"I think I'm going to be sick," said Duke. He stood up. He went to the bathroom and turned on the shower hot. The room began to steam almost immediately. Duke went to the sink and clutched it with both hands. He looked down at the swirl of painted fishes, and at a cluster of seashells that Ellie must have collected, and that she'd balanced near the faucet. He picked one up and then another.

"Ellie?" he called out. "Hey, Ellie."

Within moments, Ellie appeared by the door, wearing her thick terrycloth robe. Duke hadn't imagined she would bring that ratty ole thing from New York.

He waved at the sink. "What's all this?"

She shrugged. She looked more fragile in her robe, older. "Thought I'd make something nice. A mosaic, I don't know."

"You went to the beach?"

"You were gone so long." Ellie spread her arms open and lifted them.

"You mean you put down your laptop and phone and went to the beach?"

"I had my cell," Ellie said, turning her back on him.

"Reminds me of our girls," he said in Ellie's voice, looking into the mirror.

Right before he'd had his heart attack, Duke had seen his grandfather standing by his bed. Paw was wearing his overall and nothing underneath, his freckled chest covered with hair. He sat on a stool, with his foot straight out from under him and a hand planted on his bent knee, and said, "What does it all add up to?"

And Duke couldn't remember what he'd said, a pain in his chest like a wrench twisting his heart tighter and tighter. He could barely speak. It was lucky that Ellie had still been in the bedroom. It was lucky that she had been running late that day. Jessie was still alive, then. She'd been deployed to Iraq barely two weeks before. She had called him, long distance, while he was still in the hospital.

"Dad! What's got into you!"

"Me? What's got into you?"

"I'm helping," she said. "I've got to be here, you know that. Someone's got to."

Her voice broke up over static and echoed along the relay of satellites. It made him feel good, now, to think of Jessie's voice bouncing from satellite to satellite, floating across outer space, a sound vibration breaking up the black void.

"Promise me you'll stop drinking," Jessie had said on the phone.

Duke came out of the steaming bathroom with his hair wet and a towel wrapped around his girth. He looked at the guestbook in the living room and flipped it back to August 2013. He touched the heavy lines of the girls' scribbles on the pad, and then with his finger he traced the word, *Nana*, and then *Mama*.

Duke had come from a military family. Each of his two older brothers had gone to war. Mike had returned from 'Nam with only one arm, and Paul had his stint in Korea, and later with doctors and nightmares and pills. Both of them came back, and Duke remembered his mother in those days, lifting her arms up to God, singing at the revivals, screaming *Praise Jesus. Praise Jesus.* Back then, her prayers had made him feel light inside, tingling with the magic of God, warmed by the mercy and the Grace of his brothers coming home alive.

But when his little girl, Santa, had reclined in the hospital bed with tubes coming out of her arms, his mother had been sobbing *Jesus* into a tissue she'd pressed to her nose, and Duke then forgot all the light and music of God and could only associate from then on the smell of medicine and Santa's vomit to the words his mother muttered into the tissue, all through the chemo, all through the periods of remissions, all through the silence of Santa's hospice stay, and finally, all through the wake and funeral.

Then, there had been that black day, so soon after losing Santa, when he and Ellie had watched the Twin Towers engulfed in black smoke and collapse into a rubble. They had watched the plane fly into the building maybe half a dozen times, but each time the footage played, it made less sense to Duke than the time before.

It took about a month for Jessie to drop out of college, and then another month for her to say that she was leaving.

"I just had to do it, Dad," she said. "For Santa."

"How dare you bring Santa into this," Ellie had shouted into the phone. "How dare you do this to your father and me?"

"What does this have to do with Santa," Duke had tried to reason. "She had nothing to do with 9/11. It's insane, and you know it."

"I know it," Jessie said.

Then, she was silent, all through Ellie's sobbing recriminations, all through Duke's asking, "Can you at least try to explain? Please, Jessie, can you just try? Your mother and I have been through this thing, and now…"

Jessie had always been the sullen one. While Santa would stand on a stool in her Sunday dress to announce she was going to play at being television, Jessie could spend hours circling the same flower drawing with her crayons.

"You know what? Never mind," Jessie said on the phone, before she hung up.

But she didn't change her mind. Not through Afghanistan, nor through Iraq. She was rising in rank. She had medals. She called once per month from the desert, regardless what else may have been going on. Their conversations were always brief, to the point, and lacking in details, because of all that the army would not let her say, but before she hung up she always said, "I love you, Dad."

But Ellie never answered the telephone. Sometimes she listened in, and hung up without a word when Jessie said, "I love you, Dad."

Then, the black car had pulled up into the driveway on an icy winter afternoon, and two men in uniform and one in civilian clothes came knocking. Ellie saw them from the living room window. Duke heard Ellie cry, "Dear God," once as she rushed to the door, then cried "Dear God" into her hands a second time. She bolted the lock, just as the men in uniform knocked.

"Don't," Ellie said, with her back pressed to the door, her arms splayed open.

"Ellie…"

She shook her head and ran to the bedroom and shut the door. "Dear God, don't open that door, Duke," she sobbed. "Dear God, dear God."

It had been years since Duke had thought about God and goodness. Now he padded with his wet feet to the kitchen, saying, "I'm hungry," to an Ellie whose fingers were always clicking on a keyboard, whose eyes were always trained on a screen, and saying, "I'm about ready to go," to the two burritos and the mayonnaise and the ketchup in the fridge. He looked out the kitchen door into the screened porch, onto the hammock and the wicker chair and the blue-and-green pastel pillows and sand buckets waiting for someone to take them to the beach.

There he saw the girls again. Clearer than the last time. The younger one hopped on one foot, while the other read a book on the hammock, a foot dangling and kicking the hammock to a slow swing.

"Couldn't be older than twelve," he said under his breath.

"Did you say something?" Ellie called from the living room. He could hear her typing on the laptop.

"The girls," Duke said, not expecting to be understood.

Ellie closed the laptop with a click. Duke was pleased to see that she was dressed already. She watched a run of snowboarders while Duke slipped into his khakis and shoes. When Duke was done getting ready, an American boy was on the TV, with shaggy hair, and a big grin slashing his face in two. The kid held onto his head as his score was tallied through a loudspeaker. The boy looked stoned to Duke: he had that blissed-out stare. He moaned and groaned with the happiness of his scores.

Duke turned off the TV and together they drove to the restaurant where Arlene said they would find good food. It was cheerfully lit from the outside, an old Victorian with white pillars and a huge screened half-wrap porch. A blast of blues welcomed them. Ellie went to the bathroom, and Duke sat at the bar where deer heads were pinned to the paneled wall, and lanterns in the old-fashioned iron-wrought style hung above the liquor racks. Duke ordered a beer and a shot of bourbon. He looked up at a man-sized marlin pinned to the top of the stairs that announced new fish tacos. The music and the marlin and the girls in heels and sweaters dancing with each other by the stage made him happy.

Among the girls he recognized a familiar ponytail of blondish hair. He waved. Billy looked directly at him, but she was moving, and the music was loud, and Duke couldn't be sure what she was thinking, or if she'd even seen him. He took the beer to a table near the dance floor just as Ellie came back from the ladies' room. She eyed the beer and sat with her back to the band. She picked up the one-sheet menu and held it with two fingers and stared at him as he took a long sip.

"Vacation." He shrugged. "Just for tonight," he said.

He waved toward the girls in sweaters and boots who were dancing. One of them swapped her knees like in the twenties. "Look at that," Duke said, lifting his beer. "We could teach 'em something, old girl."

Ellie looked but she said, "Why are you drinking?"

Billy was heading to their table. Duke felt that tug in his belly like when he used to drive fast as a young man, driving the off-road tracks all full of dust, the people coming out under the stars to see the race. He got that feeling, now, looking at Billy.

"Are you listening to me?"

Ellie reached out to him and touched his arm. He pulled back just as the waitress came to the table and his abrupt gesture made him knock down his beer. The beer sprayed his pants and trickled down to the floor. He stood up, and just as the band had stopped playing, he said, "Jesus Christ, Ellie." His voice had come out to compensate for the noise of the band, and when the music stopped all that everyone could hear was Duke crying *Jesus Christ*.

"I'll bring you another," said the waitress.

"He doesn't need another," said Ellie. "One is one too many."

Billy waved, said, "Hey, Duke."

Duke said, "Sweetie, go on ahead and bring me another beer. With a shot of bourbon."

"You've got to be kidding me," Ellie said. Billy smiled with her teeth, and bounced a little as if cold, or needing to pee. She said, "Hey, y'all. Hey, Duke." She looked at Ellie and said, "Y'all enjoying Tybee so far?"

"So far," Ellie said, mopping up the beer with her napkin, "it's been cold as hell."

"Ellie, that's rude," Duke said.

"Duke was interested in ghost stories," Billy said to Ellie. The singer in the band struck a chord that reverberated throughout the restaurant, and Billy had to strain her voice to finish telling Ellie. "I told him about the house Robert Downey Jr. rented, with that grandmother who kept saying 'bout shutting the screen door." She nodded as if Ellie would understand.

Ellie had piled the wet beer napkins. The waitress had returned with another beer and a rag and she mopped off the table, telling Ellie, "Oh, I'll take care of that, dear. You just worry about having fun." And Ellie had pushed off the beer and said, "Please take that back. This man's had a stroke. He doesn't need to be drinking."

Billy pointed to her friends on the dance floor, said, "Well, I'm going to…" The rest of her words were drowned out by the opening measures of a blues song. Duke swiped the beer off the table before the waitress could take it back, and he took a long draft. He slammed the already half-empty mug on the table and pushing his voice to boom above the bass and guitar, he said, "You just mind your own business, Ellie. All you do is type on that keyboard all day. It's like being married to a ghost, it's what it is."

Ellie rolled her eyes. "Oh, Duke. Stop embarrassing yourself."

Duke nodded at her, stuffing his hands in his pocket. He nodded at her because fury would not let him find the right words to respond.

"Y'all just about ready to order?" the waitress asked.

The rage propelled Duke away from that table, away from Ellie and her clicking, which seemed to follow her even when she wasn't typing. He was furious as he padded after Billy with his hands up in the air and bending his knees to the rhythm of the music. He shook his tail and kicked out his feet and Billy laughed and danced with him, and Duke was furious. He stole a glance at Ellie, sitting alone at the table, with the stuffed moose head nailed to the wall hovering above her. Even the moose seemed happier than Ellie.

Billy sauntered up to him in a sexy shake of her bust and Duke felt that ball of fury in his chest turn into something else, something like that feeling of speed he got when riding in the truck on those speedways back home, the dust and the noise of the motors revving, and the perfect stars poking holes into that black canvas of a sky. It seemed to him that Ellie had robbed him blind. Or maybe it wasn't Ellie, but life. Life had taken the cars, the speedway, even North Carolina. It had taken his girls, both of his girls, and now it had taken Ellie, too.

Duke bumped hips with Billy and thought to himself, well, screw it! Screw it! He moved his hands over his knees, showing the other girls how to do it. He stepped on a chair and then on a table, and he waved at Ellie from the table. He put his hands on his hips and thrust up and forward and then to the side, tilting his head this way and back. He was being robbed by life, breath by breath, even now. It was as though he could feel death going through his pockets, rifling for spare change, going through Ellie's purse, too, as Ellie took the check from the waitress and looked for her wallet.

When the music stopped, the bandleader called him up on stage. Ellie lifted her face to look at him, and Duke tried to look for signs of life on her, for signs that she, too, was ready to say no to death, to stop it from sending an ice storm on their vacation. The band leader asked the patrons to give a hand to Duke, who had come here from New York, probably bringing the ice storm with him 'n' all, and Duke said he was from North Carolina, originally. New York was just a job, really, and he was glad to be back in the South.

God bless you, said the band leader.

Billy yapped and *whoohooed*, and he was buzzed, and he was hard of breath, and he was sweating, and Billy was laughing, and Ellie glowered at him, her arms folded over her breasts. Another song came on, and the girl touched his elbow and said, "What's the matter, Duke?"

"Nothing's the matter, honey," he shouted into her ear. Life's the matter, he wanted to say. Ellie's the matter. The matter is that everything dies, everything slips through your fingers and never comes back. Even when you try to come back, you never can, because you step out of time, and in stepping out of time you lose the things you had with you: what remains when you look back is just the shells, and they're broken. The building of that old school, the gym where he and Ellie met after school, the car they drove to the drive-in movie theater. Maybe if he looked hard enough he could find it, but he'd only find the shells. Time sucked away the rest. Time took everything.

But he hadn't said any of this. He'd only said something trite. Billy opened her mouth and made a funny face, squinting her eyes and dropping her jaw open as though she were laughing without sound. One of Billy's friends whispered into her ear. The two of them laughed as they looked at him.

The rhythm drained out of Duke all at once. He stood stiffly between the girls who were now bumping each other's hips. He scanned the bar for Ellie, who was dropping dollar bills on the table. He was cold, suddenly. He looked through the windows into the darkness, and then back at Ellie, who pulled her handbag strap over her shoulder and headed for the door. Billy sashayed her way to him and shouted, "Get down, Duke! Get down."

And Duke got down.

He got down on his knees.

His heart felt like a stone in his chest, so heavy and hard. His pulse felt faint, and yet, blood throbbed in his neck and at his temples. He was cold, yet his palms sweated.

"Oh, my God!" Billy cried. "Duke, are you all right? Talk to us, Duke."

The band stopped playing. A waitress and the band singer rushed to him, their hands holding him up. Duke leaned slowly backward to the floor. He was faintly aware of Ellie kneeling over him, Ellie pleading with him, "Oh no, oh please, not you." He felt her cold hands on his temple.

"They robbed us blind, Ellie dear." He was sure he'd said those words, spoken them loud and clear, but he could not hear his voice, nor could Ellie, who shouted, "Someone, please, call 911."

What he had wanted to say, at the hospital, was that he was sorry. About Billy, about his drinking again, about leaving Ellie alone to her grief, about the ice storm. What he'd wanted to say was a stream of words made of songs he'd sang as a young man, promises he'd made, to himself, to Ellie and his girls, some sunk like stones in a river, others dispersed in a breeze like the heads of dandelions.

There was no music anymore, just a buzz, a rush of sounds: the clicking of Ellie's hands on the keyboard. The beeping heart-monitor. The giggles of little girls chiming all around him. Girls in socks and T-shirts. Girls with red pails and green rakes. Girls in large beach hats, padding with purpose toward him, saying, "Come on, Daddy, let's go to the beach."

Cool sand gathered under his toes as he watched Ellie scout the shoreline plucking shells and throwing them in a bucket. She'd be sorting the striated ones from the plain ones, hoping for the occasional opalescent piece. She would set them aside for a mosaic, glue them together on a canvas, like she'd done before Jessie, before Santa. Suddenly, she seemed aware of his looking at her and turned toward him, her wet reflection in the sand stretching long behind her.

Next to her, the girls held hands, chasing the tide and laughing when the water lapped their feet. Ellie couldn't see them, of course: they were just dreams in Duke's mind. Their giggles tinkled above the sweet whisper of the surf, their young bodies light as air as they ran to him, hugged and kissed him. They lingered around for a tender moment, like an interrupted dream, then ran away again toward the sea.

ASSEMBLY HEART

The girl kept her heart in a purple velvet box by her bedside. Every morning, when she woke, she removed her heart from a latch under her ribcage, her hand reaching up into the damp warm mucus of her insides. Her long, tiny fingers, like spider hands, untwisted the cogs and mechanisms that held the heart in place until it dropped with a soft thud into the palm of her waiting hand. The girl carefully placed her heart on the velvet cushion of her jeweled box, on the bed stand. Her morning routine was fixed and reassuring. Remove the heart. Replace the latch on the opening under her ribcage. Wash the hands of the thick mucus that sealed her chest cavity. Brush the teeth. Get dressed and ready for school.

At school, the girl without a heart could then endure the long hours of Algebra class, English class, History and Spanish, the incessant droning of talking teachers enunciating, *Hoy Carlos no acabo' su tarea*, peers buzzing with gossip and boredom, the worst of it in Biology lab, where the girl dissected frogs that came in sterile, vacuum-packed plastic pouches bought from catalogs that advertised "Young Scientist Dissection Kit!" in large, cheery fonts. The girl, without her heart, did not need to consider where the frogs came from, if they were ordered via a catalog, from a company specializing in raking herpetofauna from ponds in South Carolina and Georgia, nor did she ever spare a thought for those whose job it was to fetch the frogs, knee deep in mud, from beneath the leafy greens and over fragile lily pads. She had no need to imagine the machines that shot the frogs, the fetal pigs, the lizards, and stray cats with embalming chemicals, then vacuum-packed and stacked them in airy refrigerated rooms.

At night, after dinner, after brushing her teeth and wearing her pajamas, she would reopen the latch beneath her ribcage and replace the heart inside its mechanism of cogs and screws, the girl's spidery fingers apt, after years of this practice, at screwing and unscrewing the right bolts, nuts, and washers firmly in place, while the heart continued its placid beating and pumping, as if undisturbed by her toiling, her assemblage and dis-assemblage of biomechanical complexes.

The girl dreamed of pastel rainbows and crayon-colored seas, stick-figured children chasing striated beach balls across emerald green carpets of grass. Flocks of V-birds dotted a scribbled blue sky that knew no rain, perpetually drawn to a lemon-drop sun that sweated orange and yellow lances of light. The heart, content in the dream-world of the sleeping girl at night, protected by its velvety cushions during the day, grew fat and content. Each morning, the girl noticed, the heart occupied a slightly larger space on its plush bejeweled coffer, and it would soon need a roomier box. This was especially true if, in the morning, she would try to draw her dreams with crayons on the rigidly lined notebooks on which she was supposed to write her teacher's dictations.

Sometimes the teacher's assistant looked over the girl's shoulder and cried, "She is doodling again." The other children clanged and whirred in their seats while the teacher glided over to her desk, crumpling the drawings to the rhythm of her ticking tongue. "It is forbidden to draw," the teacher explained. "Didn't you turn off your heart before you came to class?"

The girl nodded.

"Then, why do you persist with this disturbing activity?"

The girl said: "My drawing is an instinctual response to the manifestation of diverse and vivid dreams, which are themselves the manifestations of the psychic forces that are in collision or collaboration within my subconscious mind."

"Who talks like that?" the teacher ticked as she confiscated the last crayon scribble the girl had manifested on her ruled notebook, the picture of a perfect strawberry. She reported the girl to the principal's office, putting checkmarks next to "subversive behavior" and added "distinguished elocution."

The girl sat in the principal's office with her hands folded in her lap, while the principal lectured on the dangers of escapism, and his assistant tinkered with the hatch in her chest, oiling the mechanism and testing the circuitry. Still, the girl dreamed, and while she dreamed, the heart, safe in its sequined velvet box on her bedside stand, grew.

Over time, the heart would occupy a collection of jewelry boxes that grew in size like Babushka dolls, mahogany finished and scalloped bottomed, lacquered and musical, Chinese enameled and sterling silvered, gold, cameoed and mother of pearled. While other girls whose hearts, left unused, shrunk and shriveled inside the husk of a walnut, hers grew so large with her dreams that she soon rested it on a silk cushion under a bell dome, wherein the heart's ticking hummed and resounded like clinking crystals, harmonics rattling the girl's empty ribcage, loosening screws.

The dreams, too, became sonic, choirs of angels singing praise to the blade of grass, cherubs intoning canticles to sunflowers and hymns to the seafoam, vibratos that resonated across the ether. The girl slept with her forehead pressed against the glass dome, crouched, crumpled on her knees, sleep overtaking her, while the heart labored to feed itself on hers and the dreams of orphaned children, which flew like bats through the night, into the silvery spider webs that the heart's oneiric symphonies wove through the black, starless sky.

One morning, she kissed a frog-skinned boy whose hair oozed a faint scent of embalming fluid. She liked that his complexion, under the sun, glowed in a pale shade of chartreuse. It put her in the mind of an absinthe dream, in which she floated like liquor over a sugar cube and melted on the tongue of a snail. The boy and the girl held hands at recess, studied together in the library at lunch, took SATs, ACTs, and career aptitude tests on weekends. So focused on the study was the girl that she hardly noticed that, right before her eyes, the boy had turned into a lizard-skinned man, his purple tongue unfurling to catch insects, his mouth snapping shut on the small lies of his affection for her: "You are very clever" and "Your whirring is mechanically exact." When she tasted his kiss, she smelled the rain and shamrocks like the color of his eyes, but she didn't feel anything, except at night, when the heart under a pewter dome the size of a church bell unfurled crystalline odes, vitrified las and dos spewing like diamonds from a nightingale's yellow-rimmed beak. Only at night, then, could she appreciate the thrill of the boy's kiss, the thrilling novelty of a sexual attraction divorced from the mechanics of reproduction diagrammed in biology books.

She worked after school in air-sealed, refrigerated malls, serving meals assembled on Petri dishes, warmed on Bunsen burners, plucked with tweezers from fragile porcelain bowls spun out of mud, out of clay, and glazed by torch-fire. The world, she observed, heartlessly, was a dry, cracked scab pulverizing under the industrial obsession of her age, but inside the mall, as if inside the fat-heart's dream, people were swathed in cellophane wrappings, gleaming with Morse code flashes that emanated from their myriad digital portables. On break, observing the flow from the gallery at the mall, the girl experienced a most unusual occurrence—a lucid dream—a ticking in her mind that urged her to grab those crayons and paints so thoroughly forbidden to her when she was in school.

Her fingers, vine-like long, dipped into paint and traced the twine of ribbons of color, amaranth, vermillion and Venetian red, gradual shades spreading like hands on linen sheets, staining what had once been white with a prenatal vision of plasma formations. After completion, she experienced a desire: that what she had painted should be seen. After the mall closed for the night, she used her key to get in its cavernous emptiness and hung the sheets from the mall's gallery with the help of her avocado-hued boyfriend, noticing only barely that, when she had kissed him earlier that night, he had tasted like spiders.

"Why are we doing this?" he complained, his periwinkle tongue snapping, as he tapped out his repeated complaints. "This is crazy. We'll get arrested. How have you talked me into this?"

The girl remembered the principal's diatribe on the day that teacher had sequestered her strawberry drawing.

She said: "Subversive behavior is the mechanism by which the established values and principles of a system are undermined, contradicted or reversed, to protest an established social order, and its structures of authority and power." But seeing the light dimming in her boyfriend's eyes, she added. "I have tasted a variety of strawberry ice-cream flavor combinations, and it is my informed opinion that strawberry-basil is the best."

In the morning, when the mall opened, the painted sheets impressed themselves like bruises in the minds of those who beheld them, but only after the annual department mall penny-sale had concluded. Then, a woman looked up, saw the sheets and their red swirls, believed herself to have fallen into a dream, and screamed. Her toddler rose from his baby carriage and pointed, singing a melody of progressively affirmative *dah...dah...dah... dah!...* followed by a squeak.

The reaction of the patrons surrounding the woman and child seemed to progress in stages as they gradually became aware of the sheets: from their initial, self-congratulatory indifference they turned to the sheets befuddled, some crying: "It seems red, but not quite like..." and another, "Perhaps they are flowers, but inexact." There was a temporal phase of denial, when shoppers passed by the sheets with heads lowered, fists clenched and lips trapped between teeth, then a bargaining, with the store owner, with each other, though no one quite knew what agreement they were attempting to settle, then finally, all at once, there came a causeless and bewildering rage. Riots exploded. Store fronts were broken into, merchandise looted. Molotov cocktails crashed against the shields of helmeted police, flames licked at the sheets, charring them before they blazed in the glorious colors of their swirls. The wounded hugged each other, then rolled on the floor of the mall over the litter and shards of glass, crying and laughing hysterically. News channel reporters buzzed around the mall in helicopters all day, while policemen broke up the pressing crowds with cudgels and tear gas. Reporters shoved their microphones at the mouths of politicians whose eyes flashed with the clicking cameras as they tried to reassure the public that justice would be swift.

The girl watched the riot on television, while the heart pulsed safely under its dome. It had been some time since she had tried to replace that vital organ into her chest cavity, to slide it through the viscous membranes of her insides, to reconnect its cogs and mechanisms. It had grown too large, for one thing. It seemed to drain her of energies, for another. And she had grown used to the soothing rhythms of its predictable beats while she slept. But when she saw the woman with the toddler escorted to the back of an ambulance, she thought about a box large enough to contain the now exaggerated heart, perhaps a cherry-veneered coffin with a plush velveteen interior.

"Do you think we'll get in trouble?" the girl asked her boyfriend, who said nothing as he stared at the images of violence on the screen, his skin glowing a butternut yellow in the glare of the HDTV. He said nothing for a long time. Then he got up. She heard him open and close the refrigerator door. He had gone into hibernation.

The girl slept with her cheek pressed to the pewter dome, slumped against it, a trickle of saliva sliding down the curve of the heart's enclosure, the heart's rhythmic pulsing inspiring jungle dreams of tribal rituals, painted faces dancing around a pyre on a faraway beach, the slap of the waves, calling, calling.

As she slept, the SWAT team came. They came like ninjas, in black bulletproof vests and black tabi socks. They lowered ropes from the rooftop of her residence building and rappelled down to her window. Their gunshots shattered the glass, the glare of their flashlights blinding. They would hoist the heart with chains and pullies, lower it into a steel tank, torch it sealed, and bury it twenty feet deep into the ground, but not deep enough for the heart's beat to reverberate into the earth's core, not deep enough that its pulsing would not sing mysterious Irish verses to whales in the northern Pacific.

Through it all, the girl kept dreaming.

In one of those dreams, feeling the cool sand against the soles of her feet, tempted by the shock of water wetting her toes, the girl dove deep into the dream sea, into its abyss. It was a warm immersion, the waters closing instantly above her, sealing her in. She made her body into a spindle, her hands conjoined above her head, her flapping feet propelling her, and she descended with the current into the depths of the sea, the water, heavy above her, but ceding to her form as she moved. Already, through the murky green and salt-sting in her eyes, she could feel the heart's pounding sending waves that caressed her skin, then, as she grew closer, that pounding resounded inside her mechanical bones, the welcomed rattling of screws and washers tingling. She saw it then, enormous, pulsing red hot, like lava, the heart at the bottom of the abyss, crowned by the lip of a perfectly round crater, like a moon's crater; the heart contained by rock and sand. It pulsed as fiercely as ever, calling, gifting her a name, her special name, which only she could hear.

She would not have known how to stop it, even if she had wanted to, and she did not want to.

As she swam toward the crater, the heart looked larger, fierce and raw, and hungry, as it drew her in. It would devour her. She knew this as she approached. Was she still in the dream? Did it matter? The closer the heart, the louder the booming of its beat, the more her memories detached themselves from her, flakes of hopes unshared, the kisses of the lizard-skinned boy, their wet tongues sizzling like burning coals... all of it rose from her like disturbed ashes in a fireplace. The gothic spires of cathedrals she had seen in photographs, in textbooks and postcards, and the vermillion brushstroke of her sheet-painting. The words of unwritten poems in her head; the half-hummed singsongs of children playing in a park, children whose hearts still ticked undisturbed inside their chest cavities... the memories, the dreams, bubbled on her skin and detached, and swarmed into a spire, moving fast toward the beating heart. The water sizzled hot on the stone-mouth of the crater. The girl felt no fear as her hands reached the smooth, gelatin surface of the heart. The surface gave under the pressure of her hands, and her fingers slipped into the warm, sticky, viscous heart of the heart, then her wrists, then her elbows, then the crown of her head, *It smells like strawberry in here*, the girl thought, as the heart closed around the tip of her toes, and she disappeared from the world forever.

Acknowledgments

First and foremost, many thanks to Kimberly Verhines and Emily Townsend for the loving attention dedicated to this manuscript. I also want to thank the editors of the following journals for publishing some of the short stories that appear in this collection: Jon Fink of *Panhandler*, Bradford Morrow at *Conjunctions*, Joanne Raymond of *Fish Food*, Chris Tusa of *Fiction Southeast*, Valerie MacEwan of *The Dead Mule School of Southern Literature* and John Haggerty at *The Forge*. I am grateful to Georgia Southern University for the educational leave that allowed me time to work on portions of this book, and to my colleagues for their support. Also, many thanks to Myra Schoen of Willow Pond Media for her editorial insights and amazingly fast turnaround. Finally, and most importantly, I owe a debt of immense and heartfelt gratitude to my first readers, without whom none of this would have been possible: Susan Newman, Katrina Murphy, Tina Whittle, and my preternaturally patient, caring and loving partner, Joel Caplan, to whom I owe more than I can say.

photo by Joel Caplan

LAURA VALERI's debut collection of short stories *The Kind of Things Saints Do* was the winner of the Iowa/John Simmons Award, and *Safe in Your Head* was a winner of the Stephen F. Austin Press Literary Prize. A Sewanee Walter E. Dakins Fellow and a Hambidge Fellow, she lives in Savannah, Georgia, with her husband Joel Caplan. She is Associate Professor of Creative Writing at Georgia Southern University in Statesboro, and the founding editor of *Wraparound South*.